WICKED WISHLISTS

A Witch's Thrift Shop Book 3

ASTORIA WRIGHT

NOVELWRIGHT
PRESS, LLC

Cover Art by freepik
http://www.freepik.com

Published by Novelwright Press, LLC
http://www.novelwright.com

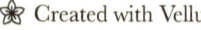 Created with Vellum

ONE

Death at Delvaux Mansion

A lice didn't usually pay attention to the newspaper vending machine in front of A Witch's Thrift Shop. Magic Row's newspapers, whose featured articles literally jumped off the pages, had startled Alice when she'd first noticed them. Once she got used to the letters and photos hovering in mid-air inside the glass case, Alice ignored them. She didn't need *"Low, Low Prices"* on brooms from The Essential Mage and didn't much care that Head Witch Charlotte Fowler was in town.

But this morning, the headline read:

"Death at Delvaux Mansion."

It not only caught Alice's attention, but her breath was snatched out of her lungs and into the cool air. The only Delvaux she knew was Sebastian, or Baz as his tenants on Magic Row called him. Baz had cast a spell on Alice the day they'd met – a memory hex. He'd accused Alice of being a non-magical person, an Untalented as the mages say, who'd wandered into the hidden world of Magic Row.

Alice could have lost all memory of herself if not for the intervention of a good-natured witch who had told Baz he was wrong and stopped his magic from harming Alice's mind.

Baz had been right, in fact, but that hadn't change Alice's opinion of him. It was his saving her life later that did that. Alice had first thought of Baz as evil, then as cold, and, more recently, as thawing like Urbana in the spring-time. Lately, Alice had begun to hope for a budding friend-ship between them.

And now that hope flitted away, along with a blue-wing butterfly that scarcely touched the metal top of the news-paper rack before Alice's outcry scared it off. She hadn't even realized she'd gasped. Alice simply hurried to the machine, propelled by the thought that the enigmatic Baz Delvaux had passed in the night.

Alice fumbled with her purse to snag a quarter, swiping her curly, black hair out of her face. She was surprised to find her hand trembling as she dropped the coin into the slot. Her reflection in the glass was pale, though, for Alice, pale was just a lighter tan than usual. Still, the face looking back at her was near panic. Did Baz mean that much to her?

She opened the case. Seizing the paper, Alice read aloud in a shaky breath, *"This morning, found dead at the foot of his bed, billionaire wizard Perseus Delvaux appeared to have been hexed."*

Alice exhaled. It wasn't Sebastian Delvaux; Baz was fine. But according to the line dancing in front of Alice's eyes, he was also a *"person of interest"* in the pending inves-tigation.

"Seems messed up." A boy's voice pulled Alice's atten-tion away from the paper. The red-headed seventeen-year-old, Puck, rested one arm on the newspaper machine while eating an apple.

"What's messed up?" Alice asked.

Puck swallowed, then pointed at the floating text. "Killing his own uncle – that's cold."

A door clattered open. Celeste, the owner of the store in front of which they were standing, appeared, holding a trash bag in hand. She dumped it into the bin between A Witch's Thrift Shop and the next building over. Then she took off a pair of blue gloves and dropped them in after. Celeste, usually well-dressed with her mid-length, black hair hugging her shoulders, had her hair up in a bun. Though she never wore tight clothing, this morning, she wore jeans and a baggy shirt as if hiding her curvy figure. She rolled up her sleeves and joined Alice and Puck by the newsstand.

"Morning. Spring cleaning, don't ask," Celeste said, putting up a hand.

"I didn't say anything," Alice replied, though she had, in fact, given Celeste a once-over.

"What's this?" Celeste glanced at the headlines.

Alice announced, "Baz is not guilty of anything." She handed the paper to Celeste, hoping her words held true. Having known Baz for less than a month, Alice couldn't be a definitive judge of his character.

As Celeste took the paper, the words switched direction to her point of view. She read the first sentence, as Alice had done, and tsked. "Shame. But I agree. Baz wouldn't do this. Certainly not for money," she said, after skimming the first line or two.

Puck took another bite of his apple, saying with a full mouth, "People do all kinds of things for money. He's already got Magic Row, but who says he doesn't want more?"

"Baz *'got'* Magic Row on his own by working hard, which you could be doing if you put your mind to it." Celeste handed Alice the paper and put a hand on her hips. "Did you steal that from Merlin's Grocery?" Celeste asked, pointing to Puck's apple.

"I got it from Many Treasures," Puck pointed defiantly at the building across the street.

Celeste turned to Alice. "Your antique store sells food?" she asked.

Alice shook her head. "He's living in the upstairs apartment with Mrs. Kinjo and Eric."

"Oh," Celeste said. For the first time since Alice had met her, Celeste looked at Puck like there was hope for him yet. "In that case, have a good day, Puck." Celeste snagged Alice's arm and led her inside.

Puck threw his apple in the trash in one shot. He wiped his mouth with his sleeve and called out, "You, too!" Then Puck winked at Hazel, the teen witch employed at A Witch's Thrift Shop, who was currently pretending to wash the store window. Hazel was still blushing when Celeste dragged Alice indoors.

"Good morning, Hazel," Alice said as they entered the store.

"Hi, what was Puck saying?" Hazel asked.

"That boy is trouble incarnate," Celeste said, storming past Hazel to the counter.

"Why? Did he say something about me? I mean, anything important?" Hazel asked, brushing her blonde hair out her eyes. The strands failed to hide her red cheeks. The poor thirteen-year-old could not hide her crush on the troublemaker in question.

"By the moon! Get him out of your mind. And you–" Celeste pointed at Alice– "Get this business in the paper out of your mind. You don't want to go anywhere near this investigation."

"Why? Did you know something about this?" Alice held up the paper.

Hazel's mouth dropped as she read the headline. A little further down the page, she gasped. "Baz killed his uncle?"

"No, he did not." Celeste stressed each word, then she took the newspaper back from Hazel. Celeste signaled with her index finger for Alice to follow her. She stopped at the front counter, where Hazel wandered around the close-by shelves and racks, pretending to be busy restocking items. Since she was most likely Untalented, having not shown a magical talent yet, she had to restock with her hands.

"What do you know about the article, Celeste?" Alice asked.

"Nothing. Except that it's bound to be spread all over town by lunch. Gossiping witches…" Celeste muttered.

"You love gossip, even if you choose not to join in. And you don't like Baz, as far as I can tell," Alice said.

Celeste snorted. "I love information, which is not the same as gossip. I like to know my neighborhood, not prey on people's reputations. And I like Baz well enough. I just wish the man forgot to collect rent once in a while. Now, let's see the rest of the article."

Alice lay the paper beside the register, where they could both lean over it and read. The words lit as their eyes traveled almost in sync down the page. The information was scarce, but not good for Baz.

"Partygoers arrived at the mansion beginning at eight for celebrations continuing late into the night. Around 1:30pm, guests had all left, according to the housekeeper, Mr. J.R. Pierce. Mr. Pierce then retired for the evening, rising four hours later to prepare breakfast for the house-

hold. At that point, only two others besides Mr. Pierce occupied the house: Sebastian Delvaux, nephew to Perseus, and Charlotte Fowler, a visiting member of the International Mage Council. Ms. Fowler arrived at 5:30 in the morning from Washington, D.C. via train.

"Mr. Pierce reports no notice of any unusual events until Mr. Sebastian Delvaux called out from his uncle's chambers, where the elder Delvaux lay sprawled at the foot of the bed. Mr. Perseus Delvaux was unresponsive to revival spells. His cause of death is unclear, but blue fingernails suggest the presence of a hex.

"Until their investigation is complete, police are hesitant to share any information on the unfolding case. One detail leaked to the public is that Sebastian Delvaux is a person of interest in the case. An anonymous tipster called into the main lines of the Urbana Police Station— bypassing the mage-only tip-line— to report having seen Mr. Sebastian Delvaux threaten Mr. Perseus Delvaux's life. Magic Row may be a motive for the murder, as Mr. Delvaux's properties are currently under sales negotiations with the store owners.

"Police continue to collect new details and leads. If you have any information pertinent to the case, call the mage tip-line directly at—"

Alice folded the newspaper, collapsing the letters in on themselves as a pair of chatting customers walked in. No need to spread the news to witches who might love to gossip. Alice lowered her voice. "You said Baz didn't inherit Magic Row from his uncle?"

Celeste smiled and waved at the two witches and then dropped her smile and voice, replying, "I don't know much about Baz, but I do know he made his fortune working for the Mage Council. And he took that fortune and bought many of shops on this street from his uncle. A Witch's Thrift Shop is one of them. Baz has owned it since I've been running it, and from rumor alone, he's a better land-lord than his uncle."

"Why is that?" Alice asked.

Celeste gave a hardened look. "For one: I've never paid protection money."

Alice's gasped "Was Perseus a-"

"Shh." Celeste's eyes followed the witches. She said, "Look, all I know is that if a level nine was killed, someone incredibly powerful killed him."

"Which is why Baz is under suspicion," Alice said.

Celeste looked back at Alice, "Which is why Baz is innocent. He would have to know he'd be the prime suspect in his uncle's death. He's too smart to even risk it."

"You have a lot of faith in him," Hazel said.

Celeste crossed her arms. "Don't you have other shelves to restock?"

Hazel set down the last of the potions she had been rearranging and turned her back to them. She walked down the row, disappearing around the corner. When she was gone, Celeste shook her head, disappointed.

Alice watched Celeste count out the days change and place it into the cash register, thinking that no amount of money in the world could have made Baz a murderer. It took her by surprise how strongly she felt. She couldn't claim she knew Baz well enough to vouch for his character, only that she had a feeling about him. She couldn't believe he was guilty.

Celeste glanced at Alice, then did a double-take. She must have seen Alice's troubled confusion. "Look, I know I give him grief about the rent and the repairs and such, but this shop would have closed three times already if it wasn't for Baz," Celeste said. As two customers walked into the shop, Celeste stopped, looked up, and smiled. When they began to peruse a shelf near the door, she continued, "I always pay my rent eventually. Baz knows it, but we've had good times and bad, and most other landlords wouldn't have let us stick around for the bad times to pass. Baz did.

His uncle wasn't like that. He had a ton of enemies, but Baz wasn't one of them. Baz never spoke an ill word about his uncle – even when we all knew he disagreed with Perseus."

"What did they disagree about? Magic Row?" Alice asked.

Celeste's eyes narrowed. "You have that look on your face - the too-curious-to-stay-out-of-it face."

"I'm just asking questions." Alice shrugged.

"No, you're not. You're solving a riddle. This isn't one of your Mysterious of the Ancient World," Celeste said.

"I – how did you–"

"I've been to your house. I saw your stack of magazines. Your curiosity is worse than your cat's, and it's almost gotten you killed a couple times now," Celeste said.

"Good thing I have a magical cat, then." Alice smiled secretly.

Celeste leaned over the counter and whispered, "Just because you have a cat-jinn, doesn't mean he can wish you up nine lives." Celeste stood up as the two witch customers wandered closer to them. Watching them out of the corner of her eye, she added, "I'm telling you, every witch and wizard in Urbana is going to gab about this story. If you get involved and make it personal, like you always do, you will be part of the gossip."

The witches walked toward them as if the word gossip was a siren call. The lure of a good story drew them to the counter. They began with a "Good morning" and drowned out Alice's and Celeste's responses by diving right into the day's headlines.

"Did you hear about Delvaux?" The woman in the purple bat-sleeve blouse asked.

The one in the leopard print t-shirt said at the same time, "Shame about Baz. You never know people do you?"

Alice slipped the paper under her arm and replied, perhaps more argumentatively than was necessary, "Sometimes we do."

The women's eyebrows raised in unison. Celeste shook her head. Alice held her chin up and gave a confident nod, showing she believed Baz was innocent. Then, she walked away, determined to prove it.

TWO

Gossip and Guffaws

Gossip spread as if by magic. By 9 a.m., it seemed like everyone on Magic Row knew about Perseus Delvaux's death. Vestra Starr, the twenty-something employee at A Witch's Thrifts shop, saw Alice in the street just outside the store. The first thing she asked was whether Alice had heard the news. Alice waved the paper in one hand as a way of saying yes.

"It's terrible, isn't it?" Vestra asked.

"Yes, it is," Alice said.

"I can't believe Baz is a killer," Vestra said in a tone that mimicked the woman in the leopard print who had said, *"You never know people, do you?"*

"I don't believe it," Alice said, tucking the paper back under her arm.

"Are you OK? You seem…upset or something," Vestra said.

Alice took a breath and relaxed. "Sorry, just Celeste telling me – never mind," Alice said, rethinking whether it was right to badmouth Vestra's boss.

"Oh, no, I get it. She's being motherly again, isn't she?

She's only in her forties and acts like we all need her advice because we're too stupid to handle our own lives," Vestra said, adjusting the bag on her shoulders so that her long blonde hair tumbled over the hint of cleavage that always managed to show– despite what she wore. Celeste was sure to tell Vestra that she'd missed a button or two on today's button-down shirt, but Alice wouldn't go there.

"Because she doesn't have one of her own," Alice said. When she saw Vestra's head tilt and her brown eyes inquiring, Alice added, "I'm sorry. I'm just upset about this news about Baz."

Vestra shrugged. "I don't know him personally."

And that was the same statement she heard everywhere. After parting with Vestra, Alice had walked across the street to Reading & Co. The bookstore's café had surprisingly good coffee and a bunch of customers spilling the tea, aka gossiping about Delvaux's death this morning. Again and again, Alice heard whispers of Baz's guilt. And over and over, she asked why no one made the presumption of innocence. The reply was a resounding consensus that no one knew Baz well enough to judge his character.

"I think it's despicable," Alice said, after she'd ordered her breakfast, she got out the word "strawberry" before the woman next to her interrupted.

"I agree. It's shameful, valuing money over his own uncle's life," the woman nodded in agreement, with several joining in on the judgment.

"No, not him. All of you. You're ready to convict Baz in a second, so you must have some pretty good reasons why you are so sure he's guilty. Right? No, your real reason is you just 'don't know him very well?' Shame on you." Alice was shaking on the inside by the time she finished speaking.

The chatter died. Every witch and wizard turned their

eyes to Alice. When the whispers started again, she had changed no one's heart. Baz's guilt made a better story to spread around the street than his innocence. But one topic was possibly more scandalous to them now. As the cashier waited for Alice to speak, the new gossip turned Alice's ears red.

Why was Alice Adelcraft so upset? Did she have some personal reason to care about Baz Delvaux? Was she involved with the wizard – even knowing he was engaged to someone else?

It didn't help that the someone to whom Baz was engaged was Titania Knight. The 5'8 heiress with golden-brown skin, a perfect hourglass figure, and long, silky, brown hair with blonde-dyed highlights put Alice to shame. At least, Alice was ashamed to think anyone compared her average 28-year-old, 5'2 body with a 24-year-old beauty queen. To a handsome, wealthy, thirty-year-old man, it had to be no contest.

The witches and wizards judging Alice now didn't say all that– at least not loud enough for her to hear. Alice only caught a snippet here or there. But, the witches' and wizards' whispers and stares said enough. It didn't matter.

Alice was not the kind of woman to steal another man's fiancé. She wasn't even interested in Baz. And she might not be gorgeous, but she was definitely "cute." She would have said so, too, if Celeste's words hadn't been ringing in her ears. *Why, oh, why had she said anything?*

Alice didn't even stay to finish her order. She turned on her heels and headed out the door, making her way to the sanctuary of Many Treasures. The antique shop wouldn't be the most comforting place in the world since witches and wizards frequented the shop. But at least it was on the end of Magic Row and back in the non-magical world on Main Street.

Right now, a judgmental cat-jinn, or genie in the form

of a cat, was sitting in the shop alongside an equally annoying store manager standing by the register. Eric Kinjo, a twenty-six-year-old future astronaut and grandson of the store's owner, often teased Alice in a younger-brother sort of way. Naveed did the same, though thankfully, he couldn't talk while in his cat-jinn form. Between the two of them, Alice would never hear the end of it if all the whispers on Magic Row spilled into Many Treasures.

The witches and wizards were wrong about Alice's reaction. Alice had not defended Baz because it was personal. It wasn't. Even if it was an emotional outburst, that didn't mean her feelings were romantic. Maybe it just hurt to think that people were quick to condemn a man just because they didn't know him. They didn't know her too well, after all, did they?

Alice pondered this as she entered the antique shop. She set her purse and the newspaper, face-down, on the front counter beside the register. Eric immediately pointed out that she was three minutes late, but Alice didn't say a word. She just hung up her coat and sat on a stool just around the counter.

Naveed, the jinn posing as a black cat, meowed as if to ask, *"Where's my strawberry tart?"* and growled as if to add, *"You promised to bring me one, and I want it."*

Eric stood at the counter opposite Alice and asked, "What's wrong? Cat got your tongue?" He chuckled as his own cliché.

Alice looked at Naveed, thinking how easily she could wish for him to catch Eric by the tongue and make the cliché literal. She sighed instead. It wasn't worth it. Eric was allergic to cats and would probably just puff up with red-buggy eyes and a swollen tongue and wheeze his complaints in her ear for the rest of the day. Alice didn't need the extra guilt.

"You'd better sit down, Eric. Stand-up comedy is not your thing. Besides, I'm not in the mood for jokes today," Alice said.

Eric sat on the stool next to Alice. His brown eyes focused on her. "Seriously, is something wrong?"

Alice unfolded the newspaper and slid it in front of Eric. Naveed jumped out of his cat bed by the window and walked over to where he could read. With a cat over his shoulder, Eric sneezed. Then he stared at the paper in awe.

After a minute, Alice asked, "You're not reading it, are you? You're just staring at the dancing letters."

"3D words? How did they do this – some kind of holographic effect?" Eric lifted the paper up and down.

Alice raised an eyebrow. "I got it at *A Witch's Thrift Shop*," she said.

"Oh, right, magic." He shook his head, adding, "I'll never get used to that."

Alice explained, "The mages– all the witches and wizards in Ur that is–all they're talking about this morning is this news."

"Who's Perseus Delvauz?" Eric asked, skimming the article.

"He's the one who invited you and Vestra to Baz's engagement party last night. It was his house – er, mansion, I guess," Alice said.

"Right. So, this Perseus guy is a wizard?"

"Yes," Alice barely contained the need to roll her eyes. She pointed to the dancing newspaper text. "And he's a businessman who owns almost all the magical property in Urbana– even a few shops on Magic Row."

"So, what do you have to do with this?"

Alice stiffened. "Nothing," she said.

"Then I say leave it alone. It's the mages' problem. Let them deal with it," Eric said.

"They're practically ready to convict Baz without a trial," Alice said.

This seemed to pique Eric's interest. He picked up the paper and stared. His eyes traveled back and forth on the page, telling Alice he was reading it in full.

After a few minutes, Eric whistled. "Killed by a hex, that's...wait, that's something they can do?" he asked. Still holding the paper, Eric began to pace back and forth. He was still wrapping his mind around the idea of magic. Weeks ago, Alice would have been freaking out the same way Eric was doing now.

Like Alice, Eric was Untalented, which meant neither of them should have known anything about Magic Row. The mage community hid street with magic. Those without magical talents, the Untalented, were never supposed to come across the spaces reserved only for Urbana's Talented members of society, a.k.a. witches and wizards.

It had been a shock to learn that mages existed, terrifying to know that they could hex Alice's memory, and confusing to learn that her own father had been a wizard. Alice placed her hand on the stone pendant around her neck. This was the most challenging part of her discoveries to explain.

Somehow Alice's Untalented mother had gifted her with a charmed stone infused with an ancient spell. The spell was unknown, and the reason the necklace would not come off was a mystery. Alice wished she could ask her parents, but Alice's mother and father had both died when she was a child. Her only hope was for Rhys Merlin, a level 10 wizard whom she'd befriended, to puzzle it out.

As if just thinking of him had conjured the old wizard out of thin air, Rhys appeared at Many Treasure's front door. He entered, holding two coffees and, surprisingly, a strawberry tart. Naveed walked back to his cot and waited for Rhys to set the tart down. He dug in immediately. Rhys smiled. Alice still wasn't sure if Rhys knew Naveed was a jinn, but as evidenced by the latté Rhys handed to Alice, he seemed to know everything.

"I forgot to order the coffee. Thank you," Alice said, taking a deep whiff of the sweet, steamy caramel scent.

"You're welcome," Rhys said in such a sympathetic way that the message Alice got from it was, *"I'm glad I could help since you seemed so pathetic while you had your mental breakdown back there."*

Alice reddened mid-sip and wiped the foam off her lips. "You probably saw what happened in Reading & Co.," she said.

Rhys had such a warm, grandfatherly smile that Alice felt her embarrassment fading. "You left so quickly I had no chance to speak with you," Rhys said.

"About what?" Alice asked.

Rhys broke off the conversation, looking at Eric. "Hello," Rhys said. His green eyes made Eric squirm in his seat.

"Uh, hi," Eric said. He had never been so tongue-tied except around beautiful girls– and apparently old wizards.

Alice almost laughed out loud. Almost. She wasn't cruel. Plus, Eric could get her back once he heard about her embarrassing moment in Reading & Co. this morning. Rhys was sure to give her away.

"Young man, would you mind allowing me a private moment with Miss Adelcraft?" Rhys asked.

"Yeah, no problem." Eric popped off his seat, ready to run up the steps.

Eric, the brave future astronaut, could sail among the stars without fear, but magic spooked him to his core. His long legs propelled him forward. Rhys stopped him with an arm.

"Just a minute," Rhys said.

"Yes?" Eric's voice held firm, but Alice could almost hear the effort it took not to quake in his boots.

Rhys held out the second cup of coffee. "For your trouble," he said.

Eric smiled, grabbing the cup. "Uh, thanks!" He said, before slowing to a leisurely pace up the staircase.

Alice had to chuckle to herself.

Rhys Merlin raised an eyebrow. "He's Untalented, am I right?" he asked.

Alice gave up trying to pretend anything with Rhys. At the same time, he had more than enough skill to hex the Kinjos if he knew the truth. "What would you do if he was," Alice answered cryptically.

Rhys put a hand up to show he meant no harm. "No hexes from me, I promise. Now, down to business." Rhys walked over to where Eric had been sitting and made himself comfortable.

"You and I both know that Baz Delvaux is not capable of killing his uncle."

"You believe he's innocent?" Alice asked.

"Anyone who knows him at all would not believe that news for a minute, as you pointed out," Rhys said.

"Seems like no one on Magic Row knows Baz well at all, except maybe Celeste," Alice said, the hope in her eyes fading.

"And you. Quite frankly, I'm glad Baz has such a fierce defender on his side. He's going to need help, especially since he's chosen just about the worst attorney to help with his case."

"Oh no," Alice said.

"Oh, yes. Tom Willows received the call this morning. Had you been in Reading & Co. a moment longer, you would have heard the news from Liza herself," Rhys said.

Liza Willows, the resident seer at Reading & Co., had a gift for telling everyone's fortune but her own. Her ex-husband, Tom, was a criminal lawyer and a cheater – in romance, if not in law. He had been representing mages for years, without knowing magic existed. When he found out that his wife was a witch, he left Liza and her two twin children, Hazel and Zade, and moved to the city limits.

If Liza's magic were not on the fritz half the time due to stress, she might have been able to see that it wasn't just the discovery of witchcraft that had sparked the move. But she had known nothing of his extra-marital affair, and it was over now. Alice had no idea if Tom intended to be faithful, but she'd grappled with whether it was right to tell Liza or not. The only thing she did know was that they were trying to make it work, and it wasn't her place to interfere with that.

And she knew that Tom's affair was with Baz's fiancé. Titania might murder Alice if she told. She might have killed Perseus, who had found out last night. How he knew about it was unclear, but Alice and Rhys had overheard his private confrontation with Titania last night.

"Given what you and I know about Mr. Willows, I would not trust him to give Baz the best representation," Rhys said.

"I wouldn't trust Titania, either. You realize she has a motive?"

"To kill Perseus?" Rhys chuckled. "Don't jump to conclusions. She's neither brave nor talented enough for that."

Alice wanted to point out that he was making assumptions himself. As far as Alice knew, Titania was as capable of killing as any magical, morally ambiguous socialite. As to ability, the means of the murder was unknown. Alice unconsciously touched the stone on her necklace as she considered how Titania might have done it.

Rhys' eyes moved to the necklace. He reached out, stopping short of touching the stone. Alice noticed him looking.

"Have any new ideas about what this is?" Alice asked, holding the stone up for him to see.

Rhys' expression fell, the bags under his eyes sagging. It was Alice's least favorite look in the world. Pity. She'd had enough of that growing up an orphan. As an adult, she tried never to give that look to others nor give others reason to use it on her. She looked away.

Naveed was the opposite of Rhys. His apathetic glare said that he'd run out of strawberry tart and might scratch someone to get it. Alice tried giving him a stern look, but he hissed.

"Alice." Rhys brought her attention back to him. "I'm going to have to leave Baz's fate to you."

"To me!" Alice said.

Rhys took Alice's hands into his own. "Baz is going to need powerful people on his side, helping to prove his innocence."

"I'm not powerful. I don't even have magic," Alice said.

Rhys smirked. "The witches and wizards of Urbana believe you are from a powerful mage family. Like it or not, you've been raised to the level of a Knight or a Delvaux. There are even some who believe you to be as powerful as a Merlin."

"As powerful as you! How could they possibly think that?" Alice shook her head in disbelief.

There was a sparkle in Rhys' eyes as he said, "It doesn't matter how the rumor started. What matters is that an Adelcraft on Baz's side – that sends a strong message."

"Except they think my motivation is—"

Rhys waved off Alice's statement before she had a chance to say it. "Your emotions for Baz are beside the point."

"I don't have any—" Alice started but was interrupted again.

"You and I know that the people closest to Baz at not the ones most worthy of his trust. If I were here, I would be the one to help Baz myself."

"But you are here," Alice said.

"Not for long, I need to find out more about your charmed stone." Rhys pointed to Alice's necklace, "Ancient, powerful magic like this is not to be taken lightly. Last week, I traveled the whole east coast searching for information on that stone, and found nothing. Last night I realized that the answer to that stone's origin is not in the United States," he said.

"Where are you going?" Alice asked.

"Better you don't know," Rhys answered.

"At least tell me when you will be back." Alice needed a little reassurance that she wouldn't be on her own.

"You can't time a task like this. It will take as long as it takes and whatever it takes," Rhys muttered. More clearly, he said, "Which is why I'm handing power of attorney over to you as a temporary measure." Rhys held a hand up as Alice began to argue. "I know I can trust you, and I can only say that assuredly about a handful of people I know."

"But you don't even know me, not really," Alice said.

"You're not talented enough – I'm sorry, but it's true – to misuse my magical possessions, and no one suspects you of murder, so you are the perfect choice." Rhys' grin gave way to a solemn, grave expression. He added, "Your father was a good man. It's strange, but I see many of his qualities in you."

"You do?" Alice asked.

"Yes, well, you're both fearless, protective of your friends, and independent."

"I'm not sure about 'independent;' I may need you," Alice said.

"You haven't needed me yet." Merlin winked at Naveed and walked out of the store.

It was true that Alice hadn't needed Merlin yet. But she also had never tried to defend a billionaire against a town of mages convinced of his guilt. It didn't seem like a difficult task. No, for a person with no magical ability, it seemed impossible.

THREE

Rousing Suspicion

It wasn't long before Many Treasures filled with mages perusing the shop. Eric returned downstairs after the tenth customer had appeared. By the time Alice saw him, she was frustrated.

"Where were you?" Alice asked.

"I wasn't sure it was safe to come down. I mean, I didn't know if your friend was still here."

"He left a half-hour ago," Alice replied.

"Excuse me if I didn't want to get hexed by a level 20 wizard," Eric said, too loud.

A witch looking at the antique necklaces by the front counter turned her head toward them with a puzzling look. Alice chuckled as if Eric had made a joke. The woman politely smiled and went back to eyeing the jewelry.

"Mage ranks only goes up to level 10 and don't make comments like that again. You'll raise suspicions," Alice whispered.

"OK, geez. I'm sorry," Eric said.

Alice realized her tone was biting, and she apologized, too. She wasn't really mad at Eric. The stares and the memory of the whispers about her emotional outburst about Baz flustered her. But most disconcerting were the glances everyone kept making when she wasn't looking. Every witch and wizard looked like they wanted to ask her a question but wouldn't dare.

Alice asked them questions instead. She found herself questioning everyone she had seen at the party at Delvaux's the night before. No one suggested any notice of foul play. If anything, they raved about what wondrous parties Perseus Delvaux threw and how sad it was that he was gone. Alice suspected those same people had hated Perseus in life.

Only one person said anything remotely helpful. "I heard Mr. Gowdie say Baz openly admitted he wanted Perseus dead," an elderly woman, dressed in layers of mismatched clothing, said. She seemed to be wearing three thin sweaters instead of one regular coat. No one seemed to care how unconventional the woman looked.

A small crowd had gathered around the cash register to hear her. Alice was the sole voice struggling against the accusations. She let the disbelief seep through her tone as she said, "I don't think Baz would ever say he wanted anyone dead, let alone his uncle."

The woman gave Alice a sympathetic look but went on with her attack. "Allegedly," she said, looking at Alice pointedly as if that word protected her from further argument. She continued, "Baz and his uncle were fighting over Mr. Gowdie's shop, one of the last on Magic Row that Perseus had not yet sold to Baz."

"I heard he's giving away all his property to some out-of-towner," someone said.

"Probably that Charlotte Fowler. She's another funny one," said someone else.

"Well, I think it just boiled Baz's blood to have any shop on this street owned by someone outside the family," said the woman who had spoken before. She glanced at Alice, adding, "Allegedly," since everyone else had said the word.

"Poppycock," a man in a sweater vest said. Alice hadn't heard that word used in anything but books, but the man seemed to be helping Baz, so she brushed off the oddness, "Rhys Merlin owns Merlin's Grocery store outright, building an all."

"Well, he's like family. You should have heard him defending Baz in Reading & Co. after, um, certain other parties said their part," the woman said.

With that, the crowd quieted down, and the stares toward Alice started up again. Alice turned away, pretending to restock something on an upper shelf behind the cash register so she wouldn't have to see them looking at her. She assumed people would continue perusing the store, but no such luck.

"So, Alice, we've been wondering…what level mage are you?" asked the woman who had looked at the necklaces. She had one in her hand now, so Alice began ringing her up. Determined to change the subject, she gave the woman the price of the necklace. The woman was undeterred. She handed Alice her a credit card while continuing, "All of us are dying to know."

Eric stepped in, "It's funny, I was just joking about that this morning. I said they ought to make a new category for her – level 20!" Eric, who could be charming when he wanted to be, winked at Alice.

Several customers began to chuckle. The woman's eyes

lit up. Her smile stretched from ear to ear. She took her purchase and her card and thanked Alice profusely before rushing out the door. Several people followed the woman, while others grinned at Alice and whispered things Alice was sure she didn't want to know.

"What are you doing?" Alice asked when the rush had died down, and the few customers left perused the books and maps in the back of the store.

"I'm taking suspicion off of you," Eric said with a shrug.

"Yes, but now they think I'm a level 10! They're going to spread that all around Urbana!" Her stomach filled with subtle variations of fear, churning nervousness into anxiety. Eric put his hand on Alice's shoulder. She expected him to say something comforting.

"You look terrible. If you're going to puke, maybe you should go upstairs and have some tea or something," Eric said.

Naveed heard 'tea' and interpreted it as 'snacks.' He rose from his perch and strutted over the counter. Eric sneezed as Naveed's black tail teased his nose. At the staircase, Naveed turned and looked at Alice as if to say, *"Are you coming?"*

The clock on the wall above Eric's head read 12:05. It was five minutes past Alice's lunch break, anyway. "Thanks," Alice said to Eric before she left. "You're such a gentleman," she added sarcastically.

Eric, grinning as he replied, said, "And yet I'm so rarely appreciated."

Alice laughed. She walked up the stairs and into the friendly surroundings of Mrs. Kinjo's and Eric's upstairs apartment. It wasn't large, but it was well furnished. Eric often complained that their furniture was old and worn, but every piece had a history. Mrs. Kinjo had a story for each one.

The coffee table, for instance, was the very first item Mr. and Mrs. Kinjo had bought together. They'd gotten it from a little antique shop just like Many Treasures. In a way, it had sparked their idea of starting their shop. The red fabric sofa was the last gift they'd received from Mr. Kinjo's mother before she died. And Alice's favorite, a small table by the kitchen counter, was imported from Mrs. Kinjo's home in Okinawa. On it sat a bonsai tree Alice had purchased this past Christmas as a thank you to the Kinjos for all the years they'd had been kind enough to let her think of them as family. Mrs. Kinjo was tending to the plant when Alice stepped into the kitchen. Naveed got to her first, rubbing up against her leg. She put her pruning shears down and pet him affectionately.

"How are you this morning?" Alice said, entering the kitchen.

Out of habit, Mrs. Kinjo went to the stove and picked up the kettle. She filled the pot with water as she replied, "Not so good. The plant is sick."

Alice walked over to it, examining the leaves. "There's still some green on the branches."

"But there are too many brown ones," Mrs. Kinjo said.

"Maybe it's not its season," Alice said. She had no idea how bonsais worked, only that Mrs. Kinjo had always wanted to try her hand at cultivating the plant. Naveed meowed.

Alice looked down to see him gesturing with his pointed ears at the plant. Alice smiled. "Maybe it could use a little magic," she said.

"Oh no, no spells. I will do this myself." Mrs. Kinjo wagged her index finger to show she was serious.

Naveed lost interest in the plant and jumped onto the

kitchen counter as Mrs. Kinjo got out the snacks. He couldn't get enough of the biscuit cookies Mrs. Kinjo always bought at the World Foods Market.

"OK, I won't interfere," Alice said. She took two cups and saucers from the cupboard and set them down of the table. Naveed floated the biscuits off the counter as soon as Mrs. Kinjo's back was turned. Alice gave him a sharp look, and a platter began to fall, she caught it quickly, then sat down before Mrs. Kinjo could come to the table with the tea. Alice set a couple of biscuits on the floor for Naveed. She held a third one in her hand, whispering, "I wish you'd stop your magic tricks in front of Mrs. Kinjo."

He bit into the biscuit ferociously. If Alice hadn't known he was magic-bound not to hurt her, she would have thought he was trying to take a finger off. Alice sat up as Mrs. Kinjo joined her at the table.

Mrs. Kinjo looked at Alice thoughtfully, tapping her chin as she said, "The bonsai was a gift from you, so if you want to help…"

"Yes?" Alice asked.

"No," Mrs. Kinjo said. "No, never mind."

"Just tell me," Alice insisted.

"Nothing. Just a bag of soil so I can re-pot if you have a chance to pick some up."

"No problem," Alice said.

Of course, Mrs. Kinjo knew that bonsai soil was not available close by and that Alice spent most of her time on Magic Row. Alice had to conclude that Mrs. Kinjo was asking if there were some type of magic soil she could use on the plant. Alice knew of only one store that might sell something like that. She'd never been to the store toward the other end of Magic Row, known as "The Essential Mage." Mr. Oliver Gowdie was the owner. Alice assumed he was the same man who was spreading lies about Baz.

When Alice finished with her tea and biscuits, she thanked Mrs. Kinjo and went back to work. She had a few hours left until the end of her shift, but then she would be free to pick up the bonsai soil. Today would be a good day to pay Mr. Gowdie a visit.

FOUR

The Essential Mage

Oliver Gowdie was a stout man with an ample belly and thinning hair. What was left of his hair was brown, except for a little patch of gray just above each ear. He wore a brown sweater vest atop a white dress shirt and striped black slacks – none of it matching. Alice wasn't sure what it was about the mage community that made them so unaware of styles. Perhaps they had a different sense of fashion.

At least most of them had a sense of decency, which Gowdie seemed to lack. When Alice walked into The Essential Mage, Gowdie stood, leaning with his elbow on a glass display-case counter, talking with a middle-aged female customer. His speech was loud and blunt as he said, "For years he's been hounding his uncle, making all sorts of threats just to get his hands on this shop."

"He knows the true value of this shop," a female customer in pretentious furs agreed.

Alice had to admit the shop had charm. The store was significantly smaller than A Witch's Thrift Shop, but they had fit a wide variety of items inside. There was only one of each item, given the small space, but they were all clearly labeled and set out in alluring displays on solid wood floors and polished cherry-wood tables.

On the right, the shop had the appearance of a high-end grocery store with barrels, carts, and table-top signs engraved with the shop's name. The items on sale looked like ones used in spells: sage, mistletoe, incense, and so on. Alice didn't see any eye-of-newt, bat wings, or any of the witchy stereotypes from TV. She did spot several magically healing tinctures, creams, and elixirs with names like CureAll Cream and *Déjà Vu* Blocker. The Cure-All might have made a good present for Mrs. Kinjo on the next gift-giving occasion if it hadn't been $60.

Alice picked up an anti-wrinkle cream but then thought better of it. As she went to put it back, another appeared. She hesitated to put back the one in her hand, thinking how she'd messed up the inventory by having two on the shelf where there had been only one. The moment Alice put the other down, however, the new one disappeared, and her problem was solved. Self restocking shelves seemed to Alice to be the best invention of magic she'd seen so far. Alice perused a bit more, listening to Gowdie while she browsed.

"No, no, Baz is not going to change a thing, mainly because he won't own this shop. Mr. Delvaux, the late Perseus Delvaux that is, God rest his soul, told me he was in the middle of a transaction of selling the shop to a woman from out of town. I don't know who this investor is, but I do wonder at the timing, with Miss Charlotte Fowler arriving in town just yesterday."

"You think Baz killed Perseus to stop the transaction?"

"Think about it; mine is the most essential shop on this street- don't mind the pun."

Using a single word from the shop's title barely qualified as a pun, Alice thought, but she continued listening.

"The Essential Mage grosses the highest income on this street and never missed a rent payment, which is more than I can say for certain other shops. Baz is netting a loss on some of the stores around here," Gowdie said.

"I can see why he'd want your shop, Olly." The woman nodded along with Mr. Gowdie.

Alice felt a surge of anger, knowing Gowdie was meant it as a jab to A Witch's Thrift Shop. She turned around quickly, too quickly. Alice gained both Gowdie's and the customer's notice as she faced them. She felt her cheeks grow red. Rather than cause another scene, she pretended nothing was wrong.

Alice walked to the left side of the shop, pretending to peruse the glass cases. This side of the store resembled jewelry counters. Under lights inside glass cases lay wands, crystal balls, and other valued merchandise. They were so new and shiny, their appearance enchanted Alice. The prices were less appealing.

Alice could see why Gowdie made a high income selling such pricey items. Did witches pay thousands of dollars for their wands?

Alice's eye was drawn to a wand with a black handle and silver and gold lines running through it. The tip looked like a diamond with several smaller gems around it. The price tag read $10,000.

Gowdie walked over to Alice. Without asking her a question, he waved a hand, and the wand came up through the glass and then back down to rest on the counter. "You've picked a beauty here," Gowdie said. He picked up the wand and pointed to the base, explaining, "This is black onyx, heat resistant so it won't overheat with extensive usage. There is plenty of gold and silver running through it for conductivity. Best of all, six different gems are attached to the center diamond, so you can channel your magic through whichever one best strengthens a particular spell."

The customer walked closer to Alice, staring in awe at the one. "A seven gemmed wand? Wow, those are rare. May I hold it?"

Gowdie set the wand down, staying, "Sorry, it's much too powerful. I'd only sell this to an seventh-level mage or higher."

"You're only saying seventh level because that's what you are, Olly. A sixth level could handle it just as well as anyone," the customer said.

"Debatable," Gowdie said. He slid the wand closer to Alice. "But in the hands of a higher-level mage, imagine what this could do." He and the customer both eyed Alice expectantly.

Alice felt tempted to try it. Part of her wanted to see what would happen with a wand in her hands. What if she *did* have powers? She knew she shouldn't believe that anymore. Alice had no reason to think anything would happen with a wand in her hands.

Still, she wanted to try. Alice brushed the black onyx handle with her fingertips. Her thumb and fingers wrapped smoothly around the cold stone. She raised it as she'd seen Baz do before.

And nothing happened.

An old fashioned bell dinged as another customer entered the shop. Gowdie and the other shopper looked up for a split second. Alice quickly put down the wand.

"I'm not shopping for a wand. I was looking for some magically enhanced soil. Do you have something that would work well for a bonsai tree?" Alice asked.

Mr. Gowdie's chubby cheeks drooped considerably, but

he nodded. Alice pretended both his and the other customer's disappointed frowns did not bother her. Let them think she had *chosen* not to use the wand.

Alice followed Mr. Gowdie to the back of the store's right side, where a few uniquely shaped desk-plants sat. There were five different colored square packets sitting side by side on an upper shelf. The writing on them was too tiny to read. Mr. Gowdie pulled his wand out of nowhere, a flashy, jewel-covered, show-off piece in Alice's opinion.

"Bonsai, you said?"

Alice nodded.

"What type of energy are you trying to cultivate with this bonsai?" Mr. Gowdie asked.

"Um," Alice hadn't meant to sound unconfident. But what type of energy would a witch bring out of a bonsai? She thought about what Mrs. Kinjo had said about why she wanted one. "Peacefulness?" Alice said. It seemed like a good guess. Mrs. Kinjo had mentioned that bonsai was used traditionally in Japanese culture to focus the mind so that it would be balanced and calm.

Mr. Gowdie sifted through the packages. "Hmm, no, this one is healing, ah, yes, here: Calming energy. That sounds about right."

He tapped the bag once with the tip of his wand. The pack began to grow. Mr. Gowdie shrunk his wand and slipped it into his pocket. Then he grabbed the bag before it became too large for the shelf. Though it hadn't actually grown further, Alice noticed as Mr. Gowdie handed the soil to her.

"That'll be $40, plus tax," Mr. Gowdie said, walking with her to the counter.

"For a two-quart bag? Alice asked.

"That, young lady, is bonsai soil. Bonsai is sensitive to magic, so the soil has to be made just right. You could try your luck with a cheaper brand, but it'll be the difference between 'don't worry' vibes and pure peacefulness."

"I wouldn't risk it. There's a vast difference in not having anxiety and being completely centered," said the lingering customer who didn't seem to be buying anything.

Alice clenched her teeth behind a smile. She reminded herself she was buying it for Mrs. Kinjo and opened her purse. As she looked down at her worryingly thin wallet, a voice passed over her shoulder.

"Excuse me," said a woman, her tone feminine and commanding.

Alice hadn't even noticed the woman who had entered the shop seconds ago. Now that she had turned around to see the woman face to face, Alice did not recognize her. The mage community in Urbana was small enough that even though Alice hadn't learned everyone's names, the people's faces were becoming somewhat familiar. This woman would stand out in any crowd.

She was thin, well-dressed in a long white coat, and her brown hair wrapped in a French twist. Crow's feet and gray hair placed her on the other side of middle-aged. Nothing in her face was particularly unattractive, but nothing was strikingly remarkable about her appearance, except her taste in clothing. Alice couldn't guess the brand of her beige business suit, but it must have been some variation of Wealth and Power, Incorporated. In her hands, she gripped a brown leather briefcase in an unbreakable hold. Her knuckles were white.

"Are you Mr. Oliver Gowdie?" she asked.

"Yes. And who would you be Miss—it is Miss, right?" Mr. Gowdie said, leaning an elbow on the counter and grinning.

The woman's upper lip curled. "I am Charlotte

Fowler," she said.

Mr. Gowdie snapped up straight. He tugged at his tie as he repeated her name, "Charlotte Fowler, as in…" His lips stopped moving unless the slight trembling counted.

Alice clutched the $40 bill in her hand so tight it wrinkled. In her other hand, the 'calming energy' plant food was doing nothing to ease the tension she sensed sweating out of Mr. Gowdie's pores. Ms. Charlotte Fowler's eyes wandered around the shop, skipping right past Alice.

"As in the new owner of this place," Ms. Fowler said. Expressionless, she peered at the wall of cabinets at the back of the store. "I need to see your backroom storage."

"I…I have a clause in the contract." Mr. Gowdie pulled a handkerchief from his suit pocket. He walked along the counter to the back cabinets, almost shouting by the time he reached the other end of the store. "It explicitly states that in the event of a change—"

"I know what the contract says, Mr. Gowdie. The fact of the matter is, I am bringing a very generous deal to you. One that would be in your best interest to take," Charlotte said.

"Is that so?" Mr. Gowdie said. Alice could see the green in Mr. Gowdie's eyes brightening with an imaginative flair.

His gaze traveled to Alice and the other customer. The female customer's eyes were wide and shining. She had *real* gossip to spread now. Mr. Gowdie wiped the sweat from his forehead.

"Well, now that I think about it, you are the new owner. It would be rude of me to refuse, wouldn't it?" Mr. Gowdie waved a hand, gesturing toward the shelves as they slid apart, revealing a thick, red cloth hanging in what must have been the doorway to the backroom.

"I'll see to this customer and be in shortly," Mr.

Gowdie said.

Ms. Fowler said nothing, simply walked to the back, turned around the counter, and disappeared behind the curtain. Alice felt the bills pulled out of her hand. She looked up to see Mr. Gowdie opening the register.

"It's forty, plus tax. You owe another $2.68," Mr. Gowdie said.

"Oh, sorry." Alice pulled another five-dollar bill out of her purse.

Mr. Gowdie counted out the difference. As he returned the difference, his hand hovered over Alice's open palm. Holding her change hostage, he said, "I hear you are backing Baz. I wouldn't place a bet like that. You'll be sure to lose." Mr. Gowdie dropped the money so that two coins missed Alice's hand completely.

Witch or no witch, Alice was no pushover. There was no way she was letting Mr. Gowdie have such a foul last word. Alice stuffed the change into her purse, all but the two pennies on the counter.

"You seem to have a strong reason to point the blame Baz's way. Even calling into a tip line, to make up that lie about Baz threatening his uncle," Alice said.

"I never called into any tip line," Mr. Gowdie remarked, angrily.

"But you did lie." Alice pushed the pennies toward Gowdie, "Anyone with two cents is going to ask the question: What do you have to hide?"

Mr. Gowdie stared at Alice as if he might curse her with her eyes. "Get out," he said.

"Gladly," Alice said, taking her time to walk out the door. She dared not show Mr. Gowdie she was anything but calm, but with every step, her heart increased its beat. Alice gripped the soil bag tightly. If its magic was going to work at all, she needed it to start with her.

FIVE

The Invitation

A lice walked out just as Baz and Titania entered The Essential Mage. Titania eyed Alice's Bonsai soil and smirked. Baz bid her good morning with a bow of his head.

"You grow bonsai?" Baz asked.

"Yes, well, no. It's for Mrs. Kinjo. She's just started growing one," Alice said, blushing despite her best efforts.

"Good for her. They generate peaceful energy that does wonders for light magic. The trick is to cast a well-being spell, not a growing spell as you would on other plants."

"You grow them?" Alice said.

"I have one in my home office. I find it keeps me centered," Baz said.

Alice smiled. Somehow that seemed just like Baz, that under his distant and unfeeling exterior was a man who tended to light-magic plants with gentle care. How Alice saw him was not reflected in the opinions of the rest of Magic Row.

As a lady and gentlemen passed by on the sidewalk, the

couple turned their noses up, a perfect angle for sticking them into Baz's and Titania's business.

"The nerve of them showing up here," said the woman, not quite in a whisper.

"Why don't you go back to your mansion, *warlock*," the man said directly to Baz.

The woman tugged on his arm, whispering, "Harold, you don't want to be his next victim, do you?"

With that, the two crossed the street. Alice could not believe the audacity of the strangers. She looked at Baz apologetically.

Baz straightened his shoulders, but nothing showed on his face as he watched them go. Titania wrapped an arm around Baz's elbow. Alice hoped it was to comfort him, but the look on Titania's face was angry...and focused on Alice.

"Good luck with your old lady's pet plant. Baz and I are picking out our engagement rings."

"Here?" Alice asked. A jewelry store seemed more appropriate.

Titania gave her a look that said, "You poor thing," and replied, "We're not going to get one that isn't enchanted with good luck."

"Household harmony," Baz corrected.

"Right," Titania grinned, "If you'll *excuse us.*" Titania pushed past Alice.

She tried to lead Baz in, but he remained where he was standing. Gently, he said, "I'll join you in a moment. I need a second with Alice."

This earned an irate look from Titania, again directed at Alice. But Titania knew better than to show her anger to Baz. She smiled sweetly, put a finger seductively on Baz's chin, and said, "Don't be long."

Her smile twisted to a grimace as she glanced one last time at Alice and walked into the shop.

"Alice," Baz said, regaining her attention. "As you may know, an associate of my uncle's, Ms. Charlotte Fowler, is staying with us."

"You can't trust her," Alice blurted. She hadn't meant to be so straightforward, but the words flew out of her mouth.

Baz blinked, pausing a moment before replying, "Trust isn't a habit with me. Why would you say that?"

"She's hiding something. I don't know what, but I'm working on it."

Baz raised an eyebrow. "You are?"

Alice suddenly felt see-through. She wondered if word had gotten to him about her outburst in Reading & Co. earlier that morning. *Oh, God, what he must think!* Alice silently panicked. She tried to keep a straight face, but it took concentration, and she missed part of what Baz said next.

"Sorry, what was that?" she asked.

Baz shook his head. "If it weren't for Merlin's intuition about people…" Baz said, as if to himself. He continued, "He seems to think you're trustworthy enough to hold his power of attorney, and since he's named in the will, I am inviting you to join Charlotte, Titania, and myself at Perseus' estate for the will reading. You would be representing Merlin and…I suppose you'd be an impartial third party, which may be helpful."

"Isn't the lawyer the impartial third party? Or don't you trust him?" Alice almost hoped he didn't. Maybe he'd replace Tom with someone else and avoid the awkwardness Alice would feel being in the same room with Tom and Titania…and Baz.

Baz's upper lip curled. "He may be impartial, but I'm

not convinced of his competence in mage law. I hear his office also deals with Untalented clients."

Alice bit back her comment. Her opinion of Baz inversely correlated to his bigotry. If she didn't adamantly believe he was innocent, she would have reconsidered bothering to defend him then and there. She couldn't stop, though; she had promised Rhys.

"I'll be there," she said, and she began to walk away.

"Don't you need to know when?" Baz asked.

Alice stepped back. "Right. Yes. When?" Alice asked, turning red.

"Tonight at 7:30pm," Baz said.

"That's fast," Alice commented.

"Charlotte insisted. She won't be in town long," Baz said.

Alice was glad of that. At least, she hoped Charlotte wouldn't be in town long enough to hurt Baz.

"Sounds good," said Alice, she waited a few seconds to make sure Baz was done, which only made it awkward as he had to move past her to get into The Essential Mage. Once she was on her way again, she took a deep breath, closed her eyes, and exhaled her embarrassment.

Unfortunately, she'd been seen. Celeste and Vestra walked out of A Witch's Thrift Shop, closing up for the day. Celeste shook her head as she locked the door. Vestra adjusted the purse on her shoulders and chuckled.

"You like him," Vestra said.

"He's engaged," Celeste reminded her. She said to Alice, "You should not be seen talking with Baz after your…moment in Reading & Co. this morning."

"Why is that? Because Baz is guilty, and I shouldn't defend him?" Alice crossed her arms.

"Yes," Vestra said.

"Not at all." Celeste gave a stern glance toward Vestra. Then she said, "Look, we're not a big community. There are maybe a few hundred of us here in Urbana. That makes us a little like a small town. Word goes around in mage circles and often sucks one down like a whirlwind with it. You don't want to be involved in this kind of investigation."

"I got involved in this community through a murder case, if you remember," Alice said.

"What do you mean?" Vestra asked.

"Never mind," Celeste said. "That case wasn't like this one. This involves members of the mage council. You don't want to draw attention to yourself by getting involved— no one does."

"True, everyone's already gossiping about…lots of things," Vestra said, not quite covering that she was talking about Alice's faux pas.

"Some are spreading news more than others. People like Gowdie are straight up fabricating lies," Alice said.

"You mean that Baz and Perseus argued? Baz and his uncle didnt get along, that was no secret," Vestra said.

"But he'd never threaten Perseus's life," Celeste said.

"It's one thing to gossip, but to call a tip-line…Gowdie is a piece of work," Alice said.

"Are you sure that was him?" Celeste asked.

"Who else would do it?" Alice asked.

"You know what I wonder? Why would any mage call into the regular tip-line? Why not call the mage tip-line?" Vestra asked. She put a hand to her chin, continuing to muse on the topic. "Someone on the mage council, maybe? They wouldn't want the tip to be traced back to them."

"Stop. If the mage council doesn't want to get involved, then you shouldn't either," Celeste said.

"The council knows Baz, they have to know Baz wouldn't kill his uncle," Alice said.

Celeste nodded. "They'll probably bring someone in to take over. Ron, too, might have to give up the case. He is the highest-ranking mage in the police department, and he can't be the investigating officer."

"Why- oh, that's right, he's Baz's future brother-in-law. That is a shame- he's probably the only one who wants to prove Baz innocent, but it makes him partial," Vestra said.

Alice glanced at Celeste. She was the only person Alice had told about Titania and Tom's affair. Alice had wanted advice about whether to tell Tom's wife, Liza, or to keep quiet as they were trying to make another go of their marriage. She was still undecided on that.

Celeste did not know that the previous night, at Baz's engagement party, Alice and Merlin had overheard a private conversation between Baz's uncle, Perseus, and Baz's fiancé, Titania Knight. Perseus had been furious to learn about Titania's affair with Tom and to Alice that gave Titania a strong motive. Though Titania's fling with Tom Willows had ended three years prior, the idea of such a scandal touching the Delvaux family was unacceptable. The uncle had threatened- no, he had decided to end the engagement.

Except Perseus Delvaux died before he could make the announcement.

Alice's stomach twisted in knots. If Baz found out about the affair and called off the engagement, would Ron still be so dedicated to discovering Baz's innocence? If Titania had killed Perseus- which Alice couldn't rule out- would he accept that possibility or refuse to investigate his sister?

Alice suspected Titania Knight had killed Perseus. Her motive? To keep Perseus from exposing her affair. Her means? She was a witch— albeit not a very good one— but she had enough powers for a hex. Presumably. Her opportunity? Titania had attended the engagement party and had even been alone with Perseus for a while.

She did it. She was the one. All Alice had to do now was connect the dots, and the mystery was over.

"Alice?" Vestra asked.

"What? Oh, right. I'm sure they'll conduct a fair investigation. I just don't see the harm in asking some people questions, too."

"The harm could be a hex on your head, and if you can't see that, you're a fool," Celeste said.

Alice knew she was talking about more than just the threat from the killer. She also meant the hex should the other mages discover Alice was not a witch. But plenty of witches and wizards were slowly finding that out, from Merlin to Vestra, and they had been supportive of keeping her secret.

"I'm not afraid," Alice said.

"Suit yourself," Celeste said, and she walked away, waving her wands and disappearing as she went.

An awkward silence lingered between Alice and Vestra. Vestra broke it by saying, "If you're asking me, I didn't see anything suspicious during the party. Eric and I were dancing most of the night. I don't think he noticed anyone but me."

Vestra may well have had stars in her eyes. That was the way of it when in a new relationship. Alice wouldn't know. She was too level headed to fall head over heels into infatuation. Instead of a *"He's the one"* feeling, the best she'd managed was a fleeting sense of *"Maybe."*

Alice wouldn't learn anything from Vestra, except that other people seemed to be happily finding their soulmates. She thanked her and turned to walk back to Many Treasures. As she took a step, Vestra's hand caught her arm. Alice turned back to see a massive grin on Vestra's face.

"Oh, I just had the best idea! Belinda was at the party taking pictures. Maybe she caught something suspicious," Vestra said.

"That's…actually a great idea. Thanks," Alice said.

"You're welcome. Wait, what do you mean *'actually*?'" Vestra asked.

Alice winced. "I meant 'absolutely.' Gotta run!" Alice said, making a quick exit.

On her walk across the street, she saw cameras flashing. For a moment, she thought it was Belinda. Fortuitous as that would have been, it ended up being a rather large crowd at Reading & Co. Alice stopped the first person she saw coming from that direction.

"What's going on?" Alice asked.

The bystander shook his head, saying, "Baz has the nerve to register his wedding wish lists all up and down this street after what he did— like he can just kill his uncle and go about his life. The press won't let him get away with that."

A plump, middle-aged woman caught up with him and grabbed his arm. She smiled at Alice, saying, "He doesn't mean anything by it. It's none of our business, is it?" She looked at the man sharply.

He straightened, "Um, yes, none of our business."

The woman dragged the man past Alice, whispering as they went, "Don't you know who that is?"

Alice felt her cheeks grow red, but not for her own embarrassment. The anger steaming in her was toward Titania. It wasn't Baz pushing the wedding. It was Titania who insisted they pick out the ring and persuaded him to set up their wedding registries. Insensitive as it was, it was not Baz's doing.

Alice looked back at Reading & Co. She wanted to go see what was happening or even to help Baz. But what could she do when she got there? Baz didn't want her comfort. Defending him further would only fuel the gossip. So, Alice walked away, feeling helpless and wondering why the whole town assumed Baz was guilty before a single piece of evidence could exonerate him.

SIX

Family Affairs

W hen Alice got home, Naveed and Puck sat on the couch, watching TV and devouring sub sandwiches.

"I thought you were with Eric working on your magic act?" Alice asked.

"Eric's got a date," Puck said.

"I'm helping the boy. I'm teaching him how to make food disappear," Naveed said.

"That's an old joke. Where does Mrs. Kinjo think you are now?" Alice asked.

"She's not my keeper," Puck said.

"She gave him a lecture after he was caught stealing from Spellbinders," Naveed said.

"Puck! I thought you were done with that." Alice folded her arms, looking like a parent.

"If you're going to lecture me, too—"

"Sit down." Alice pointed.

Perhaps because he thought she was a level-nine witch, Puck obeyed. Alice couldn't stop him from rolling his eyes, though. Since she had no experience with parenting, she paced up and down the living room.

Naveed smirked. "Are you going to say something?"

Alice put a finger up. She stopped pacing and sighed. "Can you tell me what happened?"

Puck shrugged. "I needed some stuff for my magic show."

"And you couldn't ask Mrs. Kinjo or me? Or volunteer to do some work to gain the money?"

"I needed it today, so I could practice before my audition at Grady's Bar & Grill."

"You got an audition? That's awesome!" Alice said. Then, remembering that she was supposed to be angry, she switched tone. "But you shouldn't have stolen anything."

"Mrs. Kinjo already gave me the lecture. I returned everything," Puck said.

"Good. And I think you ought to do some work at Many Treasures to make up for it."

"It wasn't even my idea! Some of my friends were daring me—"

"And if they dared you to—"

"Please don't say 'jump off a bridge.'" Puck face-palmed, as if embarrassed for her.

Alice continued, "I don't think you need to be hanging out with friends who dare you to do stupid things," Alice said.

"Relax. I scared him straight. Puck won't steal again. And, besides, he's under my tutelage now. Show her what I taught you," Naveed said.

Puck stood up, took a potato chip, and made the object disappear through sleight of hand. Alice couldn't say she was impressed, but it was definitely untalented magic and not something that would make people suspect Puck was a wizard. She gave half-hearted applause as Puck sat back on the couch.

Alice continued, "I know you're not used to someone being there for you, but you have people who care about you now. Mrs. Kinjo—"

"She's known me like two days," Puck interrupted as he gulped down the remainder of his sandwich.

"She knows me. I told her you're a good kid who needs a little help, she's the kind of person who doesn't give up on people who need her," Alice said.

"I don't need her," Puck waved the wrapper and threw the soda can into the trash can using real magic this time.

As he stood up, Alice tried again, "I'm not saying you need to be kept under lock and key, just check in with one of us so…"

"So, you can keep tabs on me?" Puck asked.

"So we know you're safe and not getting yourself into bad situations," Alice said. "This city is—"

"This city is just one place out of many I've been through. It's not my home. It's just a place to stay, and so is the Kinjos' apartment. You're not rescuing anybody, so don't pretend you are," Puck said, not even bothering to walk out the door before disappearing.

Naveed stared at Alice.

"Don't start," Alice said.

"I wasn't going to," Naveed replied.

Alice put her hands over her face and groaned. "OK, so I'm not good with kids. I just thought I could relate to him."

"You ran away from your parents, went into foster care, ran away ten more times, and filed for emancipation at 16?"

"I…what? Puck told you what happened to him?"

Naveed scratched his head, strangely reminding her of

him in his cat-jinn form. "People talk to cats, or even to familiars they think are cats. It's kind of weird, actually." He ate a handful of chips as Alice tried to process what he had said.

"So, what happened to Puck's real parents?" Alice asked.

"He didn't say. He ran away and never told anyone who his parents were, I guess no one ever figured it out," Naveed said.

"So he went into the system? It doesn't make sense. They should have been able to track his parents down," Alice said.

"These were the Untalented dealing with a wizard. He could easily have kept getting away from them," Naveed said.

"But his parents must have been mages, right? Wouldn't they have been looking for him?" Alice said.

Naveed shrugged.

"Maybe they weren't mages. Maybe they didn't know they were carrying the genes for magical abilities," Alice said.

"Or they were mages and just didn't want him," Naveed said.

Alice looked up at him in disgust, "That's horrible. I hope you didn't say that to Puck."

Naveed waved away his food. "Yes, I told Puck no one wanted him. What do you think? I'm not heartless."

"Yet you want to kill all of humanity," Alice said.

"No, I want you to be my slaves like I am yours," he pointed to the gold bracelet on his wrist that locked him into the lamp and Alice's service.

"What would you really do if I freed you?" Alice asked.

"I would rally all the free jinn of the Earth to take arms against the human race."

"So, you see why I can't free you?" Alice asked.

Naveed had no time to answer as Alice's cell phone rang. She took out her phone and hesitated as she saw the ID: The World Cultures Museum. Naveed was up and in her face in a second.

"Who is it? Why did you turn all pale like that? Oh," He said, looking at the phone.

His big blue face and black eyes stared at her in anticipation. He wanted her to take the job. He's made that clear when she had canceled the interview. Alice turned around and answered.

"Hello?"

"Alice?" a familiar voice asked.

"Yes, Mr. Coulson, how are you?" Alice asked.

"Good– better if I knew why you turned down the interview last week. I know it's not my business, but after your internship last year, we were happy to see you apply."

"I know, sir, I'm sorry for canceling so last minute."

"If another museum has made an offer–"

"No, no sir, nothing like that. It's just, I'm staying where I am for now." Alice took a deep breath. How could she explain? It made no logical sense for her to turn down a job with advancement potential and higher pay for one at an antique shop just over minimum wage. She listened to his silence and then his disappointed sigh.

"Is everything all right?"

"Yes–" Alice began.

"Because you know I didn't know your father long, but I did consider him a friend."

Alice frowned. Some part of her felt like she was betraying her father's legacy. Alice could work at the museum and still visit Magic Row, couldn't she? So why was she compelled to stay at Many Treasures?

Mr. Coulson continued, "We'd always be happy to have

another Adelcraft at our museum, but you understand that we won't always have a position like this open."

"I understand," Alice said. What else could she say? Naveed waved a hand in front of her face and gave her an eager look.

"Take the job," he mouthed.

Alice covered the receiver and gave him a look. Mr. Coulson wasn't offering her the position, anyway, just another chance at the interview; the whole process seemed like a formality at this point. She might have the job in her grasp, but she still felt so uncertain.

"If you change your mind, you're always welcome to reapply," Mr. Coulson said.

"Thank you." Alice clicked the phone off right after Mr. Coulson's reply.

Naveed had his arms crossed. He stared her down with his black eyes. At nearly 7 feet tall, the blue-skinned jinn was terrifying– or would be if he hadn't just been a furry feline an hour ago.

"Save it," Alice said.

"If you would just take the job, we could move into Merlin's Shadow. You'd have more access to the mages to learn more about your past or whatever, and I'd have a room of my own like I did at Daria's."

"I know, Naveed," Alice said. Annoyance sharpened her tone, which in turn made Naveed's voice harsher.

"Then what's stopping you?" Naveed asked.

What was stopping her? Alice didn't answer. She had no idea, but something was drawing her back not just to Magic Row, but to Many Treasures. Perhaps it was because that was where Alice belonged. Or maybe, like Puck, she'd spent a long time without a family, and Many Treasures felt like home.

SEVEN

The Reading of the Will

Last night, Baz's uncle's mansion had seemed like a fairy-tale castle. Tonight, if it was the setting of a storybook scene, it was one of the Brothers Grimm's darker tales. The weather had not warmed yet this spring, and this evening, the winds seemed to be churning up a storm.

Alice had brought Naveed with her, and she was glad when the black cat-jinn used his magic to whisk them both right to the front door. The bell summoned Mr. Pierce, the butler, who opened the door and stated in a deep baritone voice, "Ah, Miss Adelcraft. Master Delvaux and the others are in the study, follow me." He waited for Alice to step inside, closed the door, and turned as if to walk down the hallway, and then he disappeared.

Alice wasn't sure how to follow the vanishing act. She looked down at Naveed, and he meowed. Naveed pressed against Alice's ankle, and the two of them disappeared. They reappeared in a room with black leather chairs and a dark, L-shaped executive desk. A matching bookcase spanned the back wall and dancing candles— literally swirling overhead— gave an eerie hue to the colors of the book spines.

Tom sat in a seat large enough for a black-bear, of which there were three heads on the wall. It was a garish sight and made Alice feel she'd entered some twisted version of Goldilocks. One thing was clear: She did not belong.

All eyes turned to Alice. In front of the executive desk, Titania and Baz sat in two closely paired chairs. Hex stood tall on the floor beside Baz, somehow both ignoring Naveed and staring at him from the corner of her eye.

Charlotte, who sat to the rightmost side of the desk, eyed Alice in a similar expression. Her brown eyes met Alice for about ten seconds before blinking indifferently and turning back to the papers in Tom Willow's hands. It was easier for Alice to gather her courage without Charlotte's glare. She entered the room. Naveed meowed beside her, still unable to gain Hex's attention.

Baz stood as Alice walked further into the room. He gestured with his wand toward one of two chairs beside the door. The leather seat flew forward, coming to rest between Baz and Charlotte Fowler.

Alice smiled. "Thank you," she said, taking the seat he had just placed for her. Baz didn't smile, not exactly, but his lips twitched with a hint of a softer expression.

"Let's begin," Tom said, breaking the eye contact between Alice and Baz.

Lowering his wand like a cane to the ground, Baz sat comfortably back into his chair. While everyone looked solemn, no mourner's eyes held tears. It made Alice want to cry, how the closest people to Perseus, the ones to whom he had given all his worldly possessions, could listen so apathetically to his will.

"I must first point out that I am here representing my

office, as our civil law attorney is unavailable. Further, I am reading Perseus's wishes exactly as written. There is a formally written document for you all to sign, but the explanatory letter is…unconventional. You must understand that I am not adding or omitting anything past this point."

"Unconventional how?" Titania asked.

Tom flicked his eyes up sharply. "Mr. Delvaux dictated it word for word– he insisted that it not be changed." Tom loosened his tie and read:

"To the greedy bloodsuckers who have outlived me, I have no further business with you. Do not attempt a séance with me – I will not show. To the few people in this world I respect, I have given the entirety of my property.

"To Rhys Merlin," Tom looked at Alice, *"I leave everything you own to you and a word of advice: Stop hiding your treasures in other people's houses. You only put us all in danger, you old fool. I trust you to remember what you've stashed with me and expect Baz to know better than to argue with you as to what's yours.*

"To my nephew, Sebastian Delvaux, I leave my personal estate to sell or keep, though I know you don't want it. There may be some items of interest for you in the library, which I suggest you inspect before selling it all off to vultures. You may also have the building currently occupied by Spellbinders, assuming it is still in my portfolio. The split-tongued devil who owns it may have pried it out of my hands before I have a chance to update this will." Tom pulled out a handkerchief and dabbed his forehead at this point.

He knew the words he was reading were harsh, and, worse, Tom knew he was reading them to witches and a wizard. Though they thought he was a wizard himself, angering them was a bad idea. Alice hated to imagine how nervous he was feeling right now. If it had been her, her heart would probably be beating its way right out of her chest.

Tom continued, *"To the International Mage Council, I leave the property currently housing The Essential Mage in care of Charlotte Fowler, Head of Business Affairs."*

There was a bit of sweat on Tom's forehead, which Tom swept aside as his fingers brushed his hair back. He began again, *"I leave The Essential Mage property to you with the understanding that my nephew, Sebastian Delvaux, has not and will never own or profit from the building. He has agreed not to interfere nor inquire about the business status of said properties on penalty of a fine set by the owner of the buildings, not to exceed $100,000."*

Talk about harsh. Alice had never heard of such a thing: forbidding one's nephew to even ask about his property. Alice looked at the stoicism on Baz's face. Charlotte sat just as expressionless, with her head held high. Did any of these high-level mages have emotions?

What must Baz's childhood have been like to grow up with such an uncle? Or did he grow up somewhere else with his parents? He did have parents, though Alice didn't know if they were still alive. Celeste had told Alice they had prestigious titles and no jobs, living solely off wealth and often traveling when Baz was young. But Alice knew little beyond that. Her musings on Baz's childhood were interrupted by an outcry from Titania.

"There must be some mistake," Titania said. "Charlotte...she didn't even *like* Perseus."

"It's not done," Tom said. He looked pointedly at Titania.

Titania diverted her gaze to Charlotte. "Awfully convenient, you coming to Urbana just in time for Perseus' death."

Charlotte barely batted an eye. "Are you implying something?"

Titania hesitated. She was dealing with an eighth level mage, who could hex her in a second. Sitting next to the ninth level, Baz, gave her enough courage to come out with the words, "I would never dare risk your wrath."

Baz put a hand on Titania's shoulder. She quieted, though her eyes were still shooting accusations at Charlotte. Baz nodded at Tom and said, "Please continue."

Tom adjusted his tie and stretched his neck, clearly put off by the rising tensions. Clearing his throat, he resumed. "To Titania Knight, I give the requested dowry of one million dollars and the full cost of tuition for personal apprenticeship to a seventh order mage."

Titania shifted uncomfortably in her chair. Alice looked away. She remembered what Titania had told her about the pressure of living up to a perfect brother. Titania had not even reached the level of a master mage, indicating a primary mastery of magic. Given that knowledge, most would wonder how a low-level mage like Titania could kill Perseus. Alice knew from Naveed's previous owner's death that even the best mages could be caught off-guard.

Tom continued, *"That is assuming your marriage to my nephew moves ahead as planned. Should it not, the money will be held for Baz's future wife."*

Titania's flawless brown skin reddened. Her eyes flicked toward Alice, and they caught each other in a silent exchange. Titania's eyes said, *"You'd better not tell."* Alice's replied, *"I'll make that decision myself."*

Somewhere in Alice's gut, a twinge of fear reminded her that Titania may not be a master mage. Still, the fact that she had any magic made her dangerous. Alice made a mental note never to end up in a room alone with Titania. She dared not be the first to break eye contact.

Hex meowed in a gentle, almost hypnotic tone and caught the room's attention. She licked her paw gingerly, as a cat would and all returned to normal. The tension in the room was gone, and the will reading was over. As everyone else looked away, Hex caught Alice's gaze and held it. Somehow Alice understood that she was implying a need to speak to Alice.

"May you all have a long life – if not a happy one." Tom set down the paper from which he was reading. "That's the end of his letter. Now the official paperwork." Tom retrieved the documents, handing booklets to each of them. "These contain essentially the same information for each of you, though you may read them over for your satisfaction." Tom allowed them time to look over the information, taking questions from Charlotte, Baz, and Titania. It was all lawyer-lingo to Alice, so she got up to excuse herself. Hex walked to the door as if waiting for her.

At the same time, Baz stood and extended a hand to Tom. "Thank you for coming out."

Tom rose and shook his hand. "Feel free to call me if you need any help with paperwork or anything."

"I doubt that will be necessary. We…I have my own people for that," Baz said.

"And for your case," Tom began, but Baz's shoulder stiffened, and Tom stopped. Everyone, including Alice, gave Tom their full attention. He backtracked. "I will talk to you about that tomorrow. I just have a few papers for you to sign."

"I can sign them now," Baz said.

Tom grabbed a packet of papers held together with a gold paperclip and handed Baz a clear, white pen. It looked like a generic one Tom had picked up from some hotel with a rose symbol on it. Alice wondered if he was flaunting his affair, but Titania had no reaction to the pen. She was talking with Charlotte, oblivious to it. Alice held her tongue.

"I'll just gather the rest of my things and be on my way," Tom said, gathering his papers into a pile while Baz looked over the paperwork.

Alice approached the desk to say her thanks and ask Tom a question. Tom reached forward toward a flat, brown box with a red bow on top at the same time that Alice reached out to shake Tom's hand. Tom stopped and held an open hand out to the box of imported European chocolates with a tag reading *"To Perseus, Congratulations on Your Nephew's Engagement."*

"Sorry. Didn't mean to keep you from making your choice," Tom said.

"Sorry?" Alice asked.

Tom pointed to the box. "That's how Liza thinks of these. She loves chocolates, but she's got a theory on each one. The truffle goes straight to her hips, the pralines to her thighs. And don't even get her started on the caramel. Of course, nothing can lessen a woman's true beauty," Tom said, dabbing his forehead one last time before slipping his handkerchief into his pocket.

Alice smiled. Even stressed, Tom managed to charm. "I wish I could take a caramel, but that would go straight to my...well, never mind that," Alice said. She added, "I was wondering how to handle Merlin's power of attorney while he's gone—"

"Caramels were my uncle's favorite," Baz interjected. "And your pen isn't working."

"My apologies," Tom said. He took a black pen from the inside pocket of his suit jacket and reached out with his other hand for the pen. With handkerchief still in his hand, Tom took the pen like it was radioactive. He threw it in the trash as he lifted his briefcase up from behind the desk.

Answering Alice's question, Tom said, "You'll have to call my office. I'm not normally a civil attorney, I'm just filling in, as a person familiar with mage law," Tom said the last part softly. He glanced at Baz and Charlotte and looked back down at the desk, gathering the paperwork into his briefcase.

"Right," Alice said, looking down at the chocolates again. Sweets were her go-to for moments of frustration, but she resisted.

Titania spotted Alice spying the chocolates and smirked. "Go ahead and have one if you want, I'm sure Perseus wouldn't mind. And I doubt you've ever had anything so…rich," Titania's snarky tone implied a double meaning.

Alice could feel Naveed's paw on her ankle. It was his way of suggesting he could hex her anytime she gave the signal. A signal, to Naveed, could be anything, though, so Alice took a deep, calming breath. She forced herself to smile as she said, "No, thank you."

"Oh, that's all right," Titania said. Then, she turned to walk out of the study, adding under her breath, "Probably for the best." It could only be interpreted as a dig at Alice's figure.

Alice felt her cheeks grow hot, and she fought the urge to argue. For the second time that day, Alice felt like Goldilocks. Alice wasn't a size two like Titania, but she wasn't a twenty either. She considered herself to be just right for what she wanted to be, curves and all.

Alice avoided the chocolates anyway. Charlotte approached, asking Tom another question before Alice had the chance to do the same. It was something about the paperwork for the title and deed. Alice was still too angry to properly eavesdrop.

"Alice," Baz called for her attention. Alice turned to him. He held a hand toward the door, gesturing toward it.

"I can show you to the library if you'd like to collect Merlin's things," Baz said.

Alice looked around for Hex but didn't see her. Naveed was nowhere to be seen, either. Alice shrugged. "Lead the way," she said.

EIGHT

Library of Secrets

They walked down a long hallway, dimly lit, Alice was convinced, solely for an eerie effect. When they came to the end of the hall, Alice and Baz entered a large room with one wall of books filled from top to bottom. Windows spanned the wall on the opposite side of the room. A splattering of rain hit the glass panes in the dark, and the wailing of wind demanded entrance inside. Alice worried the glass might shatter, mostly because it was glowing as if illuminated by moonlight. It was magic, Alice realized. It kept the windows firm and safe from breaking.

Past the double door entrance was an executive table, which looked like it might seat twenty people, and still, the room was spacious. All the way in the back lay a coffee table, a sofa, and some armchairs. Behind it was a fireplace large enough to step into and a wall of portraits of Baz's family.

Baz walked to a picture of Perseus and slide it to the side. It revealed a safe. Baz took out a piece of paper and read some set of instructions, then proceeded to open the safe. First, he entered a combination into the lock. Next, with his wand, Baz broke some kind of spell, sealing the safe closed. The door swung open.

Baz reached inside and took out the items. One by one, he handed them to Alice, and she put them on the coffee table. Given the size of the safe, Alice was sure Baz hadn't taken out everything. But he closed the safe and sat beside Alice on the sofa.

Alice examined the contents. On the table lay a red leather book, too fancy for a journal but unmarked on the front and spine. The shiny red cover tempted Alice to pick it up.

"Merlin's things would be here. I'm not sure I remember everything that was his," Baz said, pulling the table closer.

"We could wait for him to return," Alice suggested, still eyeing the red book.

Baz shook his head. "My uncle was right. I never wanted this place. It's full of a history I'd rather not repeat. I'll be listing it on sale as soon as possible."

Alice wanted to put a hand on his and assure him that she understood what it was to have a difficult childhood. Naveed interrupted the tender moment by appearing out of nowhere and jumping on the table. Alice wished he would go away. Without being able to say it out loud, she couldn't make it an official request. Baz didn't seem to mind. He reached out for Hex, who gracefully leaped up beside Baz on the sofa. Rather than petting her, Baz slid over, letting her sit regally beside him.

Alice looked over the items on the table and smiled. "These are all unusual items," Alice said.

She reached for the object nearest to her. It was a ring with a hexagon-like symbol, only that wasn't the right description. It reminded Alice of an infinity loop, except instead of two circles extending into each other, three interlocking triangles were merging into a single shape. Alice didn't recognize the symbol. As she moved the ring closer to her face, the image changed.

"An ankh," Alice said aloud. The image always seemed to Alice like a cross, with the top of the cross forming a circle instead of a line. Life. That was its meaning. Alice recognized it from her studies of ancient Egyptian lore. It helped that she was half-Egyptian herself.

Baz looked over at the ring, which changed back as Alice turned it to show him. Baz stared solemnly at the ring as if it frightened him. He turned his eyes to Alice.

His tone was warning as he said, "That is one of Merlin's possessions. He placed the Ankh symbol over it as protection over the unicursal hexagram."

"Unicursal?" Alice asked.

Baz pointed to the triangular symbol on the ring, "That is O'Crowly's symbol. Merlin took it from his last tenth-level descendant. The ring contains warlock magic."

"Black magic." Alice gasped. The ring slipped from her fingertips. As if on cue, Naveed caught the silver, metal ring in his mouth. He set it carefully down on the table. He looked at Alice to see if she was OK.

Baz took Alice's hand. His fingers brushed her cheek. "Are you all right?" He asked. His eyes were blue crystalline orbs, and she could see into them a future clearer than any crystal ball could conjure. He leaned closer. Alice blinked, breaking the spell.

"I'm fine," Alice said. Magic lingered in the air between them, in the scent of his spicy cologne. Did he find her dollar-store, citrus-scented body spray as enticing? Alice pulled her hand away. "So, um, is this also O'Crowly's?" She pointed to a brown leather journal with the same symbol.

Baz held up the book. "Merlin has never been able to open it and has warned me against trying."

Alice caught sight of a solid black wand. It was so shiny Alice swore she could see her own reflection in it, but the image was distorted. She shuddered as she pointed to it. "And this?" Alice asked.

Baz picked up the wand, seemed enchanted by it. There was a certain sense of awe with which he handled it. "This was the wand O'Crowly used in his last battle when Merlin defeated him."

"You mean our Merlin against...what was O'Crowly's first name?" Alice asked. She'd heard of O'Crowly before, she wasn't sure where. Maybe Mrs. Kinjo had mentioned him. But O'Crowly would have lived in the 1800's and Merlin, the original, lived long before that. It couldn't have been the Merlin against the original O'Crowly, whatever his name.

Baz's eyebrows knit together, concerned. Alice had a moment of near panic, realizing any witch or wizard would probably know something about such a significant event in history. Even Naveed was looking at Alice sternly. Hex seemed somewhat amused. Would she find it entertaining when Baz hexed Alice's memory for pretending to be a witch?

"I...I know I should know this, but, see, I was raised in a slightly unorthodox way, you could say. My parents were..." Alice wasn't sure how to continue. Should she tell him she was an orphan? That might burst the whole bubble about Alice being a tenth level mage.

But Baz stopped her there. "There's no need to explain. I know the Adelcrafts have some strange philosophies on how to fit into mage society. I'm afraid it hasn't always served you well." Baz walked to a bookcase and opened a box on one of the upper shelves. It turned out to be a sewing basket, from which Baz took a cloth embroidered with Perseus' initials. "Lester O'Crowly was a descendent of the original warlock – and far worse than his ancestor. Rhys defeated him, with the help of several mage families – including yours," Baz said.

He laid the cloth on the table and placed O'Crowley objects onto it. Then, he moved on to sifting through the other objects on the table.

"Is that what your family does? Protect the magical community from tenth-level warlocks?" Alice asked.

Baz looked surprised by the question. "The council does that now. It used to be noble families, but we've progressed. One thing has always been true: Tenth-level mages are meant to protect Talented and Untalented, alike. In the case of people like O'Crowly, it's the Untalented who need our protection most."

Alice smiled. "And that's what you want to do?"

Baz stiffened. "It's not a choice. I was chosen by the council and my family. The Delvauxs are the strongest mage family left. I…it was time for one of us to have the honor of serving our community."

Alice's smile faded. Baz glanced at Alice, misinterpreting her frown. "I'm sorry, I…that was insensitive. Of course, the Adelcrafts are a strong family. I just didn't think there were any living descendants left. I'm glad to be wrong." He looked at her like that again – like he was enchanting her with his eyes.

Alice looked away. "I wouldn't want to be in your position. It sounds like a difficult job," Alice said.

"Yes…" Baz said. Then he paused, rethinking the question. He looked at her and said, "No, it hasn't been, not for a while. O'Crowly was the last tenth level warlock we know existed. With him gone, it's just a matter of catching the lower level warlocks before they can do real harm."

"And teaching the next generation to use their talents for good," Alice said.

"As I hear you are doing with Puck," Baz said. The faintest smile began on his lips, dying quickly after. "Unfortunately, there will always be warlocks around, despite your optimism."

"But not O'Crowly," Alice said.

"I wouldn't be so sure about that. The entire O'Crowly family embraced a warlock way of life. Many had to be hexed to stop them from spreading black magic through mage society. Some are still in hiding. But you are right that Lester was the only tenth level in that family to our knowledge. I doubt we have anything more to fear from them," Baz said.

"And if another tenth level warlock pops up, you'll defeat him, too. I believe in you," Alice said.

This time Baz did smile. Alice found herself blushing. She put her attention back on the table and rambled, "Who knows? Maybe one day, there will only be good magic in the world."

Baz actually laughed. "An idealist. I should have guessed that about you."

He joined Alice in sifting through the objects on the table. They both reached for the red leather book, small enough to fit in his hand. Alice dropped back, letting him take it. He flipped the page open, holding it so that Alice could see it. The first page read The Essential Mage. That was all she glimpsed of it before Baz brought it closer to him and out of her line of sight.

According to Perseus' will, Baz should have set the book down. But he turned the pages. Alice didn't blame him. She pretended not to have seen the label as he pulled the book tightly to his chest. She tried putting her mind on the rest of the items, but she Baz in the corner of her vision.

Until Alice spied a small wooden box with leaves carved in a vine-like pattern on the lid. Alice picked it up, tracing the lines with her finger until she tried lifting the lid. It didn't open. Looking closer, Alice saw it had a heart-shaped lock. She smiled.

"My father had a box like this," Alice said, tracing her fingers on the fine-grain.

Baz set down the red book, far away from Alice, and looked at Alice's new-found treasure. "My uncle's finest cigars. He kept them for moments of celebration," Baz said, holding one corner of the box.

"Like your engagement," Alice said, still holding the other end.

She mentally kicked herself the moment the words flew out of her mouth. *Why, oh, why had she said that?* The tension between them, this feeling they were sharing, eased as Baz let go.

She wanted to tell him then. It wasn't difficult to figure out why no one had seen Perseus having a cigar last night. She knew his reason for not celebrating. But telling him about Titania's affair now would be selfish.

Baz looked at the box thoughtfully. He put his hand over the lock. A soft glow pulsed beneath his fingers, and a click sounded as the lock released. Baz lifted the cigar box lid with his index finger. The disinterest on his face morphed into a narrow-eyed fascination. He clutched the cigar box firmly in box hands and stood.

"What is it?" Alice stood, too. She could not see past the lid as he held the box close to his chest.

Baz walked to the conference table and thrust the contents of the box onto the wood surface. Alice tentatively walked over to the table. She kept a distance, wary of anything that made a ninth level wizard look so concerned.

Baz's hand waved over the box's contents, scattering them in a haphazard array of pictures. They rearranged themselves into a sequence, like a storyboard. The story they told was of Titania and Tom. There were others, too. Some were of Gowdie and several other mages Alice recognized but could not name.

Blackmail photos? They didn't show enough to draw definitive conclusions about what was happening. Or they didn't until Baz set one down squarely on the center of the desk, took out his wand and shot out a spell. The photo became a moving picture – this was greater than the magic Alice had seen Belinda perform. The image had no audio, but Baz stared as if he could read their lips.

Alice wasn't able to grasp what they were saying, but she didn't need to be a lip-reader to understand the meaning of a kiss. Tom and Titania were locked in an embrace, kissing passionately on a park bench. Baz watched as if someone had pressed pause on his person. Alice couldn't read his frozen stare but imagined that it hurt to see the scene playing out.

Alice wanted to save him his pain, explain that it was three years ago, that Titania hadn't cheated on him. But some of the pictures seemed recent. Alice had seen Titania in the same dress as one of them, another in her new car.

Maybe the recent ones were pictures of them from in the meeting where Titania had pleaded with Tom to keep their affair private? Perhaps the two had been conspiring about something else, like Perseus's death. No, that would be worse.

"Alice," Baz said after a long while. "I need a moment." His voice was soft, not wavering, but not filled with the usual icy calmness. *Why could she never read his emotions?*

No matter what Baz was feeling, Alice knew she couldn't do anything to help the situation. She nodded. Alice gathered the items that belonged to Merlin in the cloth he'd set them on and left the room.

Naveed followed, and Hex soon jumped ahead of the two of them. Outside the library, Alice stopped and pressed herself against the door, finding it hard to breathe. She felt like crying.

Part of her hated Perseus for doing this to Baz. That was what Perseus had wanted, wasn't it? He'd written in his will that Baz might find something in the library. Well, he had. And…was it breaking his heart?

Alice hoped not. In fact, if she could finally admit it to herself, she was glad that he had learned the truth. Alice found her breath again and could feel the comfort of Naveed's paw on her foot.

She looked down, ready to tell him that they should go home. Then she saw Hex staring at her. Hex jerked her head back, gesturing for them to follow her. Alice and Naveed exchanged a glance and journeyed down the dark hallway to wherever Hex was leading.

NINE

Jinn Magic

H ex took them back to the study. Once she, Naveed, and Alice were all inside, Hex transformed into her jinn form. It confirmed Alice's suspicion that she was the woman Alice had seen last night, in the garden in Perseus' back yard.

Hex's skin was not blue like Naveed's, but gold. Her eyes were the same, a brilliant hue that made it an effort to look her directly in the eye. Her hair was cut short, almost Egyptian style from hieroglyphs and stereotypes on TV. Hex was tall and slender, though Naveed transforming next to her was still massive in comparison.

"You're Hex," Alice said, surprised at her own tone. It felt rude, and rude felt like a mistake when confronting a jinn. "I mean, what's your real name?" Alice asked.

Hex smiled. "Never mind my name," she said.

Hex's accent was foreign and thicker than Alice had suspected. Naveed barely had an accent at all. Alice wondered how that was possible, given how cooped up Naveed had been. Hex spent her days as a cat wandering

Magic Row. When he was with Daria, Naveed had spent his time watching TV and exercising. Yet his accent was a near-perfect American dialect. Perhaps he'd been in the US longer.

"Her name is Heketah," Naveed said, as he sat against the desk.

Alice recognized the name as close to one in Greek mythology. For all she knew, this was Hecate, goddess of magic in the ancient culture. She seemed to fit the part, even her dress was a long, sleeveless, white gown like the ones in ancient Greece. But Hex's face had traits, unlike a Greco-European woman. She reminded Alice more of an Egyptian.

Hex threw Naveed a disappointed look. "Not here. Here I am Hex, watcher of Magic Row and protector of Urbana."

"Slave to Baz," Naveed whispered under his breath.

Alice spied the amulet around Hex's neck. The color-changing gem, a fiery-red now, linked Hex to the physical world. If she were still a jinn in bondage, Baz would have kept the stone, as Alice was keeping Naveed's lamp. Then she would have been tied to him, and Naveed's words would have been true.

"I am sorry I have not yet met you properly, Alice," Hex said.

"Um…that's OK. I'm sorry, I'm still processing every-thing. I…how do you even know me?" Alice wanted to ask why Hex had chosen to give her Naveed's lamp. She wondered whether to thank her or complain.

Naveed sat with his arms crossed, pretending their conversation bored him. Hex ignored him. She took Alice's hand in both of hers.

"I know you from childhood. I watch over all the mages of Urbana," Hex said.

"You knew my parents?" Alice's eyes lit - memories kindling a fire of hope in her soul.

Hex nodded. She led Alice to a chair and pulled another one beside her. Naveed sat up on the desk, causing it to creak under his weight.

"What?" He flung his hands out as Alice looked at him.

Hex touched Alice's chin, pulling her attention away from Naveed.

"You don't remember me. But I've watched over you for a long time. I led you to Many Treasures and to Magic Row," Hex said.

Magic Row, she remembered: Hex had led Alice to the body of Naveed's previous owner. But had Hex led Alice to Many Treasures thirteen years ago? Alice didn't remember any black cats luring her places back then.

"I know that it was not an ideal way to discover your heritage, but it was necessary. You are needed in Magic Row, now more than ever," Hex said.

"But I can't help anyone. I'm not magical." Alice held up Rhys Merlin's belongings as if to demonstrate. "I don't even know what to do with these."

"They're safe with you. O'Crowly can't touch you. You're stronger than you think." Hex chuckled. She went a step far when she pet Alice's head. Now Alice knew how weird it must have felt for Naveed when Alice did that to him. At least she'd only ever done that when Naveed was in cat form.

"Um…I get that O'Crowly is dead, but what if some other warlock tries to get these?"

Hex stopped petting her head and looked at her like she was a child. "I mean that I've put my magic over you. You are protected. Have Naveed put his magic on them as well, and they will be safe in the hiding spot of your choosing."

"I don't know where to choose. Rhys didn't even keep these in his own home. He put them with you. Can't you just keep them?" Alice held the bundle toward Hex.

"They're safer with you." Hex pushed them back.

"Why? What's so special about me?" Alice asked.

Hex looked at Naveed, then back at Alice. "I can't tell you that."

"But you do know?" Alice asked.

"I think I do. Rhys Merlin will confirm it," Hex said.

"I wish he was here," Alice said.

Naveed stood up.

"She doesn't mean that literally. It's not an official wish. Sit down." Hex waved a hand, and Naveed sat, as if on command.

"You need to teach me how to do that," Alice chuckled.

"She doesn't have control over me," Naveed said.

"I am a jinn of the air, and you are a jinn of fire," Hex said.

"I," Naveed sounded like he wanted to argue, then realized what she said. He scratched his head, mumbling, "That's right."

Alice couldn't help the hint of a smile creeping into her lips. She knew from Mrs. Kinjo's interest in jinn that those of the air were more powerful than those of fire. It was best for Naveed's ego if he didn't realize that. Hex didn't outright explain it, either.

"Can you tell me anything? About my parents? About me? Why did you bring me to Magic Row? Why do I have this?" Alice pulled the charmed stone out from under her neckline.

Hex held a hand over Alice's, pushing the stone back. "I can only tell you that everyone thought it safer to keep you out of Magic Row, away from your magical heritage.

But I disagree. You won't bring about our destruction. You will be our salvation."

Naveed hopped off the desk, this time looking determined. "What do you mean, "our salvation?" The magical community?" He pointed at Alice skeptically, "She's a threat to them?"

"There has to be some mistake," Alice said.

Hex stood, her eyes flashing gold. "I make no mistakes. If I say anything, the future changes. But you are important, Alice. Powers or none, and I have faith in you."

Naveed laughed uproariously. He threw in a head shake and an eye-roll, too. Alice glared at him, then sighed as the weight of Hex's words lost their gravity.

Alice gave a wry smile. "I'm glad someone has faith in me," she joked.

Hex remained solemn. "Those who don't will see their error soon."

"What do you mean? How soon?" Alice asked.

But in the space of a second, Hex walked to the door, opened it, and transformed. Her black cat-jinn form left the room and disappeared down the hall.

"See? I told you she was a drama queen," Naveed said.

"No kidding," Alice whispered.

She looked at the desk, deciding the chocolates might be worth it after all, but the package was gone. It figured. Alice barely had the strength to feel disappointed. She handed Rhys's journal, ring, and wand to Naveed.

"Let's go home," Alice said.

TEN

The Butler's Beliefs

A shadow appeared halfway down the hall, causing Alice practically to jump on Naveed's tail. He leaped aside and hissed. Mr. Pierce rounded the corner to the site of a cat barring its teeth and ready to attack.

"Shh," Alice said.

"Is everything all right?" Mr. Pierce asked.

"Yes, we're just leaving," Alice said.

Mr. Pierce nodded. "I'll show you out. Right this way."

Naveed growled. His tail lashed out at Alice's ankle. Alice flinched and turned around, making sure she hurt Naveed.

"I'm sorry, OK? I didn't even step on your tail."

He hissed again.

"I wish you'd stop," Alice whispered while trying to follow the butler.

Naveed obeyed, joining Alice and Mr. Pierce down the hall. Mr. Pierce turned around.

"Is there something wrong, miss?"

"Oh, no…just a little jumpy, I guess, you know, with all

this talk of death and will readings. I don't suppose you have any of that chocolate left?" Alice joked.

"Chocolate?" Mr. Pierce asked.

"The box you set out for the will reading," Alice said. Mr. Pierce raised an eyebrow, seeming genuinely perplexed. "Never mind," Alice said.

They took a few steps in silence. When they reached the foyer, Alice noticed the fresh-cut flowers on a table by the door.

"Those are beautiful," Alice said.

"They're from Mr. Smythe, from Spellbinders," Mr. Pierce said. He pointed to another bundle across the foyer in the living room. "Those are from the Knights." As he pointed out the various flowers from sympathetic mages, Mr. Pierce pulled out a handkerchief. He dabbed his teary eyes."I'm sorry, I don't mean to be emotional," Mr. Pierce said.

Alice put a hand on his shoulder. "It's difficult to lose someone you care about."

"I suppose. I never thought I'd actually miss the old man." Mr. Pierce paused at the front door. "Old man" was ironic, coming from Mr. Pierce. Seeing Alice's sympathetic stare, he explained, "Perseus was harsh, and not always the easiest to work for, but he took care of his own. He paid for my wife's funeral, got my son into a good school. I'm not sure what I'll do now that he's gone."

"I'm sure Baz will take you on," Alice said.

"Unless he's in jail for Perseus' murder. He's not guilty, but I suppose you already know that," Mr. Pierce said, smiling as he folded up his handkerchief and put it away.

Alice looked down. Everyone in town seemed to know about her defending Baz at Reading & Co. She cleared her throat. "Um…about that. Do you have any idea who might have been involved in Perseus's death?"

"There's a long list. I don't know who specifically, but you might start on Magic Row," Mr. Pierce said.

Alice remembered what Celeste had told her. "Did he really take protection money from some of the shop owners?" Alice asked.

"You've been talking to Gowdie? It's not true. Gowdie likes to say that since Raj Smythe bought the Spellbinders building, Perseus started hounding Raj for protection money, but both Perseus and Raj denied it. Gowdie just likes to keep tongues wagging. It gives him more business when people think they'll get the latest gossip from him."

"Did Perseus ever threaten Gowdie, with a libel lawsuit or anything?" Alice asked.

"I don't know. But if you're thinking Gowdie killed him, he'd have to have been in two places at once. He went out drinking after the party 'till late in the morning. And I heard he was making up stories about Baz and his uncle arguing until well past 1am."

"So, you can confirm Baz and his uncle weren't fighting?" Alice asked.

"They don't always see eye to eye, but Baz would never hurt his uncle. Family means everything to Baz, even more than his own happiness," Mr. Pierce said.

"I see." Alice wasn't sure Mr. Pierce meant it that way, but Baz's engagement came to mind. She had a feeling Baz had only agreed to marry Titania to fulfill his uncle's wishes. Perseus had practically said that to Titania. Would he break the engagement now that he knew about her affair?

The thought of the photos Baz had found sparked a realization. It wasn't protection money Perseus had been gathering. It was blackmail. Perseus must have had a stockpile of secrets to use against the mages of Urbana.

That made the list of suspects long, but it also made it

easier to trace. All Alice had to do was narrow down the people in the photos in the cigar box. She turned to trace her steps back to the library.

"Miss Adelcraft?" Mr. Pierce asked.

"Oh, sorry, I left something in the library," Alice said.

"Perhaps we can return them to you tomorrow?" Mr. Pierce asked. He explained, "Baz has asked to be alone."

Alice paused. She felt Naveed's tail curling around her ankle. Turning back to the door, Alice nodded. "Tomorrow would be fine," she said as Mr. Pierce opened the door.

Naveed transported them home magically. Alice immediately went to the fridge and took out the orange juice. Her hands felt shaky, and the magic travel always got to her. A few sips later, she felt better and noticed Naveed back in jinn form, pacing the room.

"I saved you that chocolate you wished for," Naveed opened his palm to show her a caramel from Tom's chocolate box.

"Ugh. Not after orange juice, thanks," Alice said, holding her stomach.

Naveed dropped the chocolate onto the counter. He walked over to the couch and sat down. Alice expected to hear the TV, but after a minute, the living room remained silent. Alice turned to see Naveed on the sofa chair, staring at the window.

"What's wrong?" Alice asked. There was a long list from which to choose, the primary problem being Baz's situation. Alice hoped Naveed was close to a solution.

But no, he wasn't even thinking about Baz.

"She thinks she's stronger than me?" Naveed asked.

"Who?" Alice asked.

"Hex," Naveed said. "Fire jinn are just as strong as air jinn." He scratched his head.

"And twice as temperamental," Alice muttered before taking another sip of juice.

Naveed whipped around. "We're passionate," he said. Then, he flopped his massive blue body onto the couch.

"Sure," Alice put her glass into the dishwasher and walked into the living room. "Why not channel that passion and help me find out who might have killed Perseus?"

Naveed waved a hand, batting away the notion. "Humans are always killing humans, who really cares?" he asked.

"You're in a mood. Why are you so angry at us, anyway? And don't tell me it's because you're bound by your lamp, you know I'd free you if I trusted you the way Baz trusts Hex." Alice sat next to him on the couch.

Naveed remained silent.

"I wish you'd tell me," Alice said gently.

Naveed's jaw dropped in shock and indignation. Alice put her hands up.

"No, that's not an official wish. I'm just interested as your friend," Alice said.

Naveed took a deep breath, the kind that hitched like he'd just been stabbed by emotion. His dramatic pause had Alice on the edge of her sofa-seat.

"Humans like your friend, Eric, want to reach out into the stars. They say they want to know they're not alone, but since the world started, humans have never been alone. There were other human-like people on the Earth."

Alice nodded. She knew from all her studies about Cro-Magnons, Neanderthals, and all the species that came before modern man. She couldn't see what Naveed was getting at, though.

He continued, "There were also jinn. We were not

violent. We stayed within mist and fog watching and weeping when we saw the violence between physical beings. Humans were the most violent of all. They wanted to dominate the world, and they succeeded."

"How old are you?" Alice asked.

Naveed tilted his head, giving her a look as if he was disappointed at her straying thoughts. He responded curtly, "I'm not saying I was there. I know the stories."

"So, you're saying all jinn hate all humans because we used to be violent?" Alice asked.

She knew that wasn't true. There couldn't be a shared cultural hatred of humans among the jinn. Hex didn't hate humans, and she was a jinn.

"Never mind," Naveed said. He reached for the remote.

Alice's voice softened. "I'm sorry," she said.

Naveed flipped through the channels, ignoring her. Alice stood up, walked over, and stood in front of the TV. He tiled his head, looking past her.

Alice threw her hands up in the air. "Come on, Naveed, I'm trying to be your friend," she said.

"You can't be my friend and my master, it doesn't work like that." Naveed clicked the remote again.

Alice sighed. That was a fair point. But Alice had made the same argument again and again. "The only person keeping you enslaved is you. I can't trust you not to destroy the world, so I'm not letting you go free. I think, if you're honest about it, you know that's why Daria didn't free you, too. It's not our fault that we can't trust you."

"You need me to keep pretending you're a witch," Naveed said.

"Yes, I do. And Baz needs Hex to help him protect Magic Row, which she does of her own free will."

"Then, she's still as much a slave."

"She's bound, all right– by her own kindness. She's there for Baz, and he's there for her because they share a bond. That's friendship. You could give that a try, Naveed."

"With you?" He asked.

"With me, with Puck, with Eric and Mrs. Kinjo, with whoever you want. You know in your heart that they only want your happiness. I think if you're honest, you want them to be happy, too. I don't think you have it in you to hurt them."

"Then why not free me?"

"Because right now, you're convinced that you don't care about any humans. You need to figure out how you really feel."

"I could just pretend to like you all," Naveed said.

Alice stood up, saying, "You'd rather pretend to be a cat, remember? And besides, you're not that good an actor. Puck found you out in a second."

"He still doesn't know I'm a jinn," Naveed said.

"And he can't find out. No one can," Alice said.

"That will be difficult with you going around asking questions about the death of a powerful wizard. And now you've got those in your hands." Naveed pointed to the magical objects on Alice's coffee table.

Alice frowned. She should have left them with Baz. Given his emotional state, Alice hadn't wanted to ask him any favors. Hex had said she'd protect the objects with magic, and Naveed had already used his magic on them.

"What spell did you use?" Alice asked.

"Jinn don't use spells. I put some of my magic on it to keep it from leaving this apartment." Naveed said it in that condescending tone he used whenever he had to explain basic facts about magic to Alice. Jinnsplaining. So annoying.

Alice learned quickly, though. "Put an extra spell...I mean more of your magic on it to keep anyone but Merlin from using it," she said.

"What if you to use it?" Naveed asked.

"It's black magic, even if I could, I wouldn't. And no, you can't use it either," Alice said the second Naveed started to ask.

"Where do I put them?" Naveed asked.

"I don't know. Can you put them in your lamp?"

"Only I can fit in my lamp, and even then, it's a cramped space," Naveed grumbled.

"OK, so...I don't know. It has to be a place no one would think to go into, like the cabinet above the fridge. Or a place no one sees, like the air vent behind the hamper," Alice suggested.

"You're asking me to decide?" Naveed asked. He looked around the room thoughtfully. A few seconds later, he waved a hand, and the objects disappeared.

"Done," he said.

"Where did you put them?" Alice asked.

Naveed held a finger up, waving it. "Uh-uh. It's better if you don't know."

"Yeah, you're probably right." Alice stood, stretched her legs, and said, "I think I'm going to call it a night. I'm wiped out."

Naveed pointed a finger at Alice, and her clothing changed into her blue pajama t-shirt and pant set. She frowned. Alice knew it wasn't the same as someone changing her out of her clothes; it didn't involve Naveed touching her, let alone seeing anything. Still, she hated the idea of surprise dressings and undressings. Naveed only did when Alice said she was exhausted, but she'd explained to him before that she could do it herself.

Tonight, she was too tired to argue. "Thanks," she said, and she wandered off to her room. By the time she brushed her teeth and wandered over to her bed, she was sure she'd fall asleep before her head hit her pillow.

But she tossed and turned, thinking about everything that had happened and hoping Baz was all right. Alice lay on her back, looking up at the ceiling, then turned to her side, then onto her stomach, searching for a comfortable position. When that didn't work, she fluffed the pillow.

Something moved. Jumping up from the bed, Alice lifted the cover to see the wand roll toward her. Lifting the pillow revealed the journal and ring, too.

Alice marched out of the room and over to Naveed, who still watching TV on the couch.

"My bed? Really?" Alice held the pillow in one hand and the wand in the other.

Naveed shrugged. "You said a place no one would think to go, and no one ever sees. It fits the description."

"Very funny," Alice said in a voice that indicated she was not, in the least bit, amused. Alice went back into her room, flopped the pillow onto the bed, and grabbed the journal and the ring. She walked into the kitchen and slid one of the kitchen barstools over to the fridge. Alice hid the objects herself on the cabinet above the refrigerator. Naveed sat uselessly watching her.

When she'd finished hiding the objects and dragged the chair back into place, she turned to Naveed. "Tomorrow, we're going to call Rhys and ask him what he wants us to do with his things."

"You can't call him," Naveed said.

"What?" Alice was so tired, she wasn't sure if it was

true that she didn't have his phone number. He'd given her one, hadn't he?"

"Merlin only has a landline at the apartments and his grocery store. He doesn't use technology otherwise."

"Great," Alice said, putting her hand to her forehead.

"You can still contact him," Naveed said.

"How?" Alice asked.

"Same as any well-trained witch would: Crystal ball."

ELEVEN

Crystal Ball Communication

For mages who did not own their own crystal-based communication devices, there were always fortune tellers. It wasn't what they were trained to do, but it was, as Celeste informed Alice the next morning, a service they could provide. So, instead of purchasing her own crystal ball for Naveed to use, Alice and Naveed walked down the street to Reading & Co.

She was early, as Liza was just setting up for the day's readings. Liza had just lit the incense when Alice tapped on her open door. Seeing Alice, Liza smiled and threw away her match.

"Hi, Alice! Good morning, Fluffy." Liza bent down and petted Naveed from head to tail. He seemed to enjoy it when she did it. He always hissed at Alice. "What brings you here this morning?" Liza asked.

"I was wondering if I could contact someone real quick?" Alice asked.

Liza glanced at a flower inspired clock above the door. "Oh, I have another reading in a half-hour. How long has the person been dead?"

"No, not dead. This one is alive. It's Rhys Merlin. He's out of town, and I thought—"

"Oh, say no more. Sure, you can! I'll leave the room and give you some privacy." Liza started walking toward the door as Alice walked in.

"Thanks," Alice said.

She noticed as Liza walked by that her face was slightly puffy under the eyes. The minute she was out the door, Alice asked Naveed, "Did she seem all right to you? I think she's been crying."

Naveed jumped onto the table where the crystal ball sat and looked at Alice, with a reproaching glare.

"OK. I get it. I'm coming," Alice said.

She sat in what must have been Liza's chair, a little afraid to put her weight on it. The chair was antique-looking, a thin woven twine with arms and legs that looked like they might not stand much pressure. Sitting in it, Alice was surprised that it felt sturdy and comfortable. Alice turned her attention to the crystal ball, which looked like a regular see-through orb to Alice.

"What do I do?" Alice asked.

Naveed meowed. He placed his paw on the crystal and stared into the ball. Alice watched and waited. A few seconds in, Naveed made a sound an awful lot like sighing. He cocked his head and twitched an ear at Alice.

"Oh, you want me to put my hands on the glass? Well, you should have said that."

Naveed growled.

"Calm down. I'm doing it," Alice said.

She put her hands on either side of the glass, her right hand pressing down alongside Naveed's paw.

Naveed meowed. Somehow Alice understood.

"Um, Rhys Merlin, please?" Alice asked.

Nothing happened. Naveed meowed again, this time

more forcefully. Alice sat up straighter, gazed deeply into the glass, and tried again. "Rhys Merlin."

A glow began to radiate from Naveed's paw over the surface of the whole crystal. Like a rippling wave, the appearing image was difficult to see. As the wave calmed, the picture became clear.

Rhys Merlin's face appeared in the ball. Alice jumped back, almost letting go of the crystal. Rhys' face was pressed up close, his pointed nose prominently displayed inches from Alice's face.

"Alice?" Merlin asked.

"Yeah–yes, it's me."

"What's wrong? Has something happened."

"No," Alice answered. She took a breath and relaxed her fingers. This wasn't so hard, Alice thought. She could get used to it. Alice continued, "The will reading was last night."

"So soon? Vultures. I'll bet that wasn't Baz's idea."

"Charlotte was mentioned in the will. She wanted to settle things before she leaves town."

Rhys nodded, which amounted to his nose, moving up and down, providing a closer view of his nostrils than Alice would have liked. Her lips pulled back of their own will. Alice tried to turn a grimace into a smile. She was pretty sure she looked like she was in pain.

"What happened?" Rhys asked.

Now she was up close and personal with one of Rhys' eyes. Alice gulped. She re-interpreted the question as being about the reading of the will.

"Perseus left you your own things you were keeping in his vault. A journal, a ring, and–"

"The wand," Rhys said.

Alice nodded.

Rhys' lips came into view. "You must return the wand.

Do it today. The journal and the ring are of less significance, but if that wand falls into the wrong hands…" Rhys did not finish the sentence. The imaged moved up and down over the whole of Rhys's face. He looked more troubled than Alice had ever seen him.

"There is some jinn magic on it, protecting it," Alice said. She didn't specify whether it was Hex's or Naveed's magic. She still wasn't sure he knew she had a jinn of her own.

"Good. That's good." Rhys said. Thankfully, the image had stabilized, and now Alice could see all of Rhys Merlin's face. He continued, "Still, it shouldn't be left outside of a mage-brand safe. A ninth level mage can protect it better than you. I'm sorry, Alice. That's just the truth of it."

"I understand," Alice said.

"Keep the wand with you until you can take it to Baz's new home. Put the items in Baz's safe and have him seal it with his and Hex's magic."

"I will," Alice said. The picture began to distort. "Rhys," Alice called out. His face appeared again.

"I've just arrived at my destination, Alice. Is there something else? I'm afraid I haven't got much time." Either it was Alice's imagination or Rhys looked worried.

Alice wanted to tell him that Baz had found out about Titania's affair, but there wasn't anything Rhys could do about that. Alice had nothing else that absolutely needed to be discussed.

"No, stay safe," Alice said.

"Yes, yes. You too," Merlin said. That was his goodbye.

The image rippled again, and then it was gone. Alice looked at Naveed. "I guess we go back to see Baz," she said.

Naveed meowed and leaped down from the table. Alice

stood up from the chair. She looked at her watch: 8:38am. Alice had about twenty minutes before she had to get to work. It wasn't enough time to go see Baz and get back, even with Naveed's magic to instantly transport her there. It was enough, though, to find out what was wrong with Liza.

Pulling the door open, Alice found Liza seated at a table by the window of Reading & Co.'s café. She had a magazine open and was flipping through the pages when Alice sat down opposite her. Naveed jumped into the empty chair beside Liza, startling her.

"Oh! Hey, are you all finished?" Liza smiled. She instinctively began petting Naveed, who once again just purred and settled into her touch.

"Yes, thank you," Alice said. As Liza began to stand, Alice put a hand up. "Wait, Liza, do you have a minute?" Alice asked.

Liza sat back down. "Sure. What's wrong?"

"That was my question. Are you OK?" Alice asked.

Liza looked down and fiddled with the corner of the magazine cover. "Is it that obvious?"

"Maybe just to people who know you. I mean, I haven't known you long, so maybe I don't have a right to say that," Alice said.

"Oh no, some people just have connections. I felt that way when I met you like we were friends in another life," Liza said.

Alice smiled. She wasn't sure she believed in all that, but then, she hadn't thought magic existed three weeks ago. "Ditto," she said. "So, do you want to talk about whatever is bothering you?"

Liza sighed. "It's Tom."

Alice felt her stomach twist. Even Naveed twitched an ear. Baz had only found out about Tom and Titania last night. Alice couldn't believe that Baz would tell anyone about the affair, much less mention that the married man Titania had been seeing was Tom.

But Liza wasn't raging about it, she had a sort of nostalgic smile on her face. The knot in Alice's stomach relaxed as Liza continued, "It's been great having Tom back with us. These last few days have been a dream for the kids. Seeing their father again has made Hazel so happy, and you should see Zade, spending every minute he can with him. It's like we're back to how it was before. Tom has even talked about moving us in with him."

"You're leaving Merlin's Shadow?" Alice said.

Liza looked away. She folded her arms, and Alice could see her tensing up. She waited for Liza to continue. Finally, Liza said, "The problem with things feeling the same as before is that it's all *too familiar*. Toward the end, it was like he was keeping secrets from us and now…" Liza wrapped her arms around herself. "It's the same. He still blames me for keeping my Talent a secret, I can tell. But it wasn't like I was trying to keep a secret from him. He just – didn't believe in any of it."

"But you think he's purposely keeping something from you now?" Alice asked. She had to know what Liza knew or at least suspected.

After a long silence, Liza laughed. She shook her head and smiled at Alice. "It's probably just my imagination. Everything is fine." Liza sounded like she was saying that more to herself than to Alice.

And Alice felt like a rotten friend for not having told her about the affair. She might find out about it anyway, especially if the two hadn't broken it off. If they were still seeing each other, as the recent pictures suggested, wouldn't it hurt less hearing it from a friend than some other way?

"Liza," Alice said.

Naveed meowed, catching Alice's attention. "Yes?" Liza asked.

Naveed shook his head. He didn't want her to tell? But why? Alice couldn't argue with a cat and certainly couldn't just ignore his advice. Plus, her own nerves were glad for an excuse to get out of telling.

"Never mind, sorry. I have to go, but we'll talk later, OK?" Alice asked.

Liza nodded. "Thanks," she said as they both stood up. She pulled Alice in for a hug, catching Alice by surprise. Then, she walked into the reading room to start her divinations.

"I feel like a monster," Alice whispered only loud enough for Naveed to hear.

He meowed nonchalantly, then hopped off the chair and began walking to the front door. Alice followed him to the alleyway beside Many Treasures, looking left and right. No one lingered outside this early, and Alice only saw one person in Many Treasures with his back to the side window. Looking down at Naveed, Alice said, "Go fetch the bag with O'Crowly's items and take it directly upstairs. Not in front of Mrs. Kinjo, or you'll give the poor woman a heart attack."

Naveed nodded and disappeared. At roughly the same time, Eric opened the side door.

"Hey, you've got a visitor," Eric said.

"Me?" Alice asked.

"Yeah, the museum guy," Eric said, opening the door for Alice to step inside.

TWELVE

A Museum Proposal

"Mr. Coulson?" Alice asked, seeing the brown-haired man looking over the trinkets at the front counter.

"Alice! It's good to see you," Mr. Coulson said. He set down a Civil War-era lighter and met Alice halfway inside the shop. Eric wandered somewhere out of the way. Alice was too busy paying attention to the old man in the striped pin-suit shaking her hand. He always looked the same, no matter how far back Alice remembered him. Slim built and tall, a slight black beard, dark hair, bright, blue eyes, and a smile that welcomed everyone into his museum. His friendly demeanor made it hard to say no to anything he asked.

Nevertheless, Alice shook her head. "Mr. Coulson, I already told you I can't take that job-" Alice began.

"I'm not here about a job. I just wanted to make sure you and the Kinjos are OK. I just realized how long it's been since I've seen Eric. And how amazing he's turned out, already an astronaut!" Mr. Coulson grinned in Eric's direction.

At the back of the store, Eric held a hand to the back

of his neck. "Not yet, I don't graduate till the Fall semester, and then there's the acceptance into the training program…" Eric realized he was rambling and blushed. But Mr. Coulson looked genuinely impressed as he replied, "It's just a matter of time."

Mr. Coulson walked with Alice to the counter, where she walked around the register and set down her purse. Sighing contentedly, Mr. Coulson remarked, "Time is a funny thing, isn't it? This neighborhood used to be something great. Now, I've been hearing about strange things going on around this street."

"Strange things?" Alice held her breath.

"Yeah, I heard there was a shooting a couple of blocks from here," Mr. Coulson said.

Alice let the breath go. "Right. That was terrible," Alice said, recalling just the prior week when mage officers caught a vandal who had been causing chaos on Magic Row. It had been wand-fire, not gunfire that landed two wizards in the hospital, but the Untalented neighbors couldn't make sense of what they'd heard. As far as Alice knew, no one had actually seen anything.

"It seems like this neighborhood is becoming a dangerous one," Mr. Coulson lamented as he looked out the front window.

"I agree," said a man who must have entered through the side door directly facing Magic Row. The man, brown-skinned with gray at his temples and wearing a plaid suit, walked up to the counter, squeezing right past Mr. Coulson. He asked Alice, "Do you sell wands here, or perhaps a ring–something that conducts magic?"

Mr. Coulson raised an eyebrow and gave Alice a skeptical look.

Eric walked over to handle the customer's request.

"No, sorry. We don't carry those, but we've got a tarot card set if you're interested."

"Tarot? What would I do with a tarot card set? I'll just browse a bit," the man said, wandering to one of the back tables.

With a *"see what I mean"* expression, Mr. Coulson said, "Alice, I'm not just saying this because your father was the curator. You were the most promising intern we've ever had. Are you really going to spend another year, or waste another day, in this place?"

"I'm happy here," Alice said, biting back the uncertainty she felt bubbling up in her stomach. She hoped the fear and anxiety she felt carrying the burden of O'Crowly's possessions wasn't showing on her face. But, if she was honest, she was feeling overwhelmed this morning.

Eric seemed to notice her distress. He came closer to the counter and addressed Mr. Coulson. "If you want to check on my grandmother, I'm sure she'd love to see you. She's upstairs."

Mr. Coulson nodded and smiled, then found his way to the stairs and walked up. As soon as he was gone, Eric raised an eyebrow at Alice. He gave her that look he used whenever he called her bluff. Alice didn't like it any better than Naveed's judgmental expressions.

"What?" Alice asked.

"You know, Grandmother and both couldn't understand why you gave up that job interview."

Alice shrugged, "What's to understand? I like it here."

"Alice, all you talked about for years was working at that museum. Now you're not interested?"

Alice gestured with an open hand toward the alleyway. "In case you hadn't noticed, there's a real-life magical world outside our door."

"That doesn't change the fact that this is still just an antique shop," Eric said.

"That's not the way your grandmother thinks about it. These are treasures that your dad and grandfather collected. They should mean more than that to you."

"Oh, they do, but they're not keeping me from following my dream. The question is: Do these antiques really mean so much to you that you'd want to stay in this shop forever?"

"I didn't say forever," Alice said, but Eric ignored her.

He continued his thought without hearing her. "Because it seems to me that you're staying so that you can keep pretending to be something you're not and missing out on what you're really meant to be."

Alice bit her lip softly. Was that what she was doing? Alice felt her cheeks reddening. Being overwhelmed turned into a general confusion with just a touch of anger. Why was Eric suddenly making good points about Alice's life instead of sitting there with a nose in his books? Wasn't it her job to point out that he was missing out on life?

Eric put a hand on Alice's shoulder. "We just want you to be happy. I'm going over to Vestra's. Just think about it, all right?" Eric smiled. Then he walked toward the side door.

"Wait a second. It's Monday. We're supposed to redesign the front window display this morning. I'm not doing it by myself."

"Don't worry, you won't be doing it alone. I got you a helper. I think I hear him coming down right now." Eric said as he walked into Magic Row.

Naveed came downstairs, meowing. He jumped up on the counter and lazily curled up into his cushion. Naveed's relaxed demeanor told Alice he'd hidden O'Crowly's possessions well and was sure they'd be safe until lunchtime. Alice wouldn't feel right until she and Naveed returned them, or until Mr. Coulson left.

Puck trampled down the steps behind Naveed.

"All right, what are we doing?" Puck asked, more enthusiastically than Alice expected.

"Eric hired you to redo the window display?"

"He hired me to help *you* do it. So," Puck took out his wand and pointed at the window. The antiques in the shop window – a lamp, a mannequin boasting a Victorian-era dress and jewelry, a standing mirror, and a small writing table with several trinkets – changed places.

"There! Are we done?" Puck asked.

Alice rolled her eyes and walked over to the window and put a hand on Puck's, "Not even close. And we get Untalented customers, so, please, no magical displays."

"Still as spirited as ever. That woman never ceases to amaze me. Why, what's this?" Mr. Coulson said as he walked toward the front of the store. He eyed the wand curiously.

"It's magic," Puck said, grinning at Alice as she gave him a stern look.

"He means it's an illusionist's gimmick," Alice said.

"Ah, you're a magician?" Mr. Coulson asked.

It was Alice's turn to smirk. Puck flicked the wand into his sleeve so quickly, it really did look like a magician's trick. Mr. Coulson clapped.

"Bravo," he said.

"Thanks. I'll be doing shows soon. I'm thinking of the stage name *Puck, the Wandering Wizard,*" Puck said.

"Where do you perform?" Mr. Coulson asked.

Puck shrugged, "Nowhere yet. But I'll be booked some-where soon."

Mr. Coulson took out his wallet and handed a card to

Puck. "Perhaps you could perform a show at the museum."

"Really?" Puck said, taking the card.

"Why not? Magic has been a part of the Urbana folklore for a century. And with antique wands and crystal balls and such, we could incorporate a little history into the show."

"That's not a wand. We don't sell things like that here," Alice said for the umpteenth time, though it was the first time she'd said it to an Untalented.

"Isn't it?" Mr. Coulson asked.

Puck sat on the chair behind the counter, not looking Mr. Coulson in the eye as he lied. "It's just a twig."

"Oh, no matter, I'm sure you have some other trinkets that carry superstitious origins here." Making one last attempt to sway Alice, Mr. Coulson stopped at the door. He turned to Alice and said, "I can see why you're drawn to this place. I'm sure you saw right through me about my reason for coming here today. I am here about an offer, but when I said it wasn't about the job, that was true. There's a new position involving some travel, a paid internship this time. You'd be working with me, personally, in Egypt. If you're interested, call my secretary, and she'll tell you the details." Mr. Coulson handed her his card.

Alice wasn't sure what to say. Opportunities like this were rare. It seemed like a no-brainer that she ought to say yes. Instead, she said, "Thank you. I'll think about it."

"That's all I ask." His smile widened as he turned and walked out of the shop.

"Nice guy," Puck said, flicking the card between his fingers. He had his feet up on the counter near the register. Alice tapped his shoe twice.

"Up. Come on, let's get to work on that window," Alice said.

Puck hopped off the stool and headed to work. Before Alice turned around, Naveed meowed. He was grinning at Alice like he'd found a million dollars. Alice shook her head. "I didn't say I'd take it. I'm just going to think about it," she said.

Naveed's smile disappeared. He dropped his head, laying back down in his basket and gave a low, guttural growl.

He could sulk all he wanted. Alice wasn't sure she wanted to be anywhere but Many Treasures. Yesterday she was sure she only wanted to be here. Today she had to admit she was enticed by the idea of Egypt. A research trip, probably the same kind of travel her father had done when he'd met Alice's mother. Connections to the past were hard to pass up.

As another customer entered the shop, Alice slipped Mr. Coulson's card into her pocket. Alice smiled at the customers, two witches heading straight for the jewelry and a wizard browsing the old maps.

She'd memorized those maps by heart. Now, she might have the chance to travel to places on the parchments like Egypt. Merlin was there, somewhere near Cairo, searching for information on her necklace. The thought turned her stomach. She couldn't think about silly adventures when he was on a dangerous mission for her sake.

Alice had to keep her attention on what she needed to do for Merlin. O'Crowly's possessions needed to get back to Baz today. It was time to forget about Mr. Coulson, and focus on her duty toward Merlin, and Baz, and the people of Magic Row. Eric was wrong. She might be pretending to be a witch, but she had become a part of the mage community. Alice couldn't help but feel that even if she took the job with Mr. Coulson, she was meant to be a part of Magic Row.

THIRTEEN

Breakups and Break-Ins

Alice expected to see Baz disheveled and heartbroken. Instead, he was dressed in his usual business clothes, looking immaculate and well-composed as ever. He answered the door himself or at least opened the door from the other side of the living room with the wave of his wand. Alice spotted him immediately, sitting at a table by the fireplace. He set down his wand without looking up and kept looking over documents and books. The red book, in particular, sat open in front of him. He closed it as Alice neared.

"Miss Adelcraft, I didn't expect to see you today."

"It's Alice, remember?"

The slightest smile adorned Baz's face as he said, "Alice."

Whatever spell Baz had over her sparked something magical in Alice's heart as he said her name. Still, she wasn't sure how appropriate it was to be feeling such things. For all she knew, Baz was still engaged.

"I expected you to still be at your uncle's," Alice said.

She caught sight of Hex entering the room. Naveed

walked past Alice toward her, and the two cat-jinn settled on the rug by the fireplace. Naveed leaned into Hex's shoulder, but she sat stoically with her eyes locked on Alice. Baz took Hex's entrance as a cue and offered Alice a seat on one of the sofa chairs. He took the one opposite her.

"I had intended to be out of that house yesterday if events had gone differently." Baz's eyes drifted a moment. Alice imagined he was thinking about what might have happened if his uncle had not been killed. Baz cleared his throat and continued, "In any case, the home already has a buyer."

"Who?" Alice asked.

"Charlotte Fowler. The council has offered her a job here. She and I are finalizing the deal on the home tomorrow morning," Baz said.

"That's a surprise," Alice said. Vestra's words came back to her. Maybe she had a point about a member of the council not wanting to use the mage tip-line. Except Charlotte hadn't been in town earlier in the night, so she couldn't have reported Baz's argument with his uncle.

"Not so much a surprise as a secret," Baz replied.

"A secret?" Alice asked, her mind still wondering if Charlotte hadn't called the tip-line anyway, just to lie about an argument that never happened.

"Urbana is full of secrets. Or haven't you noticed?" Baz said, looking into the fire. His icy stare froze on the flames.

"It's full of gossip, too. Like that libel about you're threatening your uncle."

Baz turned his blue eyes to her. "It's true."

"It can't be," Alice said, her voice barely rising above a whisper.

"I did threaten to end his life in Urbana, by exposing his secrets. I knew he was blackmailing people. I wasn't sure how, but I knew at least one person whom he was threatening."

"You blackmailed him about blackmailing people?"

Baz smiled. "Yes, I see the hypocrisy. I was trying to change him, not kill him," he said gently.

"The cigar box with the blackmail pictures in it. Could one of them have wanted Perseus dead?" Alice asked.

"All of them probably did, but I can't see any of them actually harming him. Even Gowdie would not poison a man," Baz said.

"He was blackmailing Gowdie, too? Wait a minute, Perseus was poisoned, not hexed?" Alice asked.

"Cyanide, a rather mundane method of attack," Baz said.

"Non-magical," Alice remarked.

"Yes, a very clever way to avoid an M-trace and hide a person's level of Talent," Baz said.

"Someone is setting you up," Alice said.

"It would seem so," Baz replied.

She got the impression from Baz's thin-lipped frown that she shouldn't ask further. Instead, she slipped the tote-bag off of her shoulders. "I came to return these to you," Alice said, sliding to the edge of her seat with the bag in her outstretched hand.

Baz reached out and held the tote open in front of him. "O'Crowly's possessions?" he asked.

"Rhys thought they'd be safer with you," Alice said. Then, realizing that might make him question her magical status, she added, "He mentioned you have a secret safe in a hidden library. That's safer than an apartment, right?"

Baz regarded her with kind eyes, then looking deeper into the bag, he asked, "Was there a reason for not including the wand?"

Confusion passed over Alice's face. Hex jumped onto Baz's sofa chair, looking over his shoulder into the bag.

"It should be there." Alice looked at Naveed, whose pointed ears twitched as he looked between Alice and Baz.

"Have you left this out of your sight?" Baz asked, standing up.

"I…it had magic on it for its protection. I was sure it was safe." Alice stammered she walked close enough to look into the bag.

Baz reached out a hand, stopping short of Alice's shoulder. "I'm not blaming you. We need to narrow down who might have had taken it."

"You think someone stole it?"

"If you haven't misplaced it, and I'm assuming you haven't, what other explanation is there?" Baz asked.

Naveed growled, and somehow Alice understood that he agreed with Baz.

"Think, Alice. Who might have had access to it?" Baz asked.

Alice adjusted her glasses, looking nervously at Naveed. A list of names came to mind. Mrs. Kinjo, Eric, Puck, even Mr. Coulson had gone upstairs where Naveed had stashed the items for just a couple hours. But they weren't mages, except for Puck, and he wouldn't have any talent stronger than Naveed's jinn-magic. Of course, any number of customers might have been able to make it upstairs without Alice noticing. Still, they wouldn't have known O'Crowly's wand was in the apartment.

"There was one customer," Alice said, recalling the man who had asked for a wand earlier. "But I don't think he would have had access to it. He left right away."

"Just because a customer asks about a wand means nothing," Baz said.

"He asked about a wand *or a ring* – that's pretty specific, isn't it? It was almost like he knew both of those were right above his head in the upstairs apartment."

"Only the wand's owner would have been able to sense it. But perhaps he knew something about the will and your role in handling Merlin's affairs. He might have spelled himself upstairs without your noticing. What did he look like?" Baz asked.

Alice shook her head. "I don't know. An old man – no, a middle-aged man with gray at his temples. I don't remember exactly."

"There's only one way to know for certain. We'll have to do an M-trace on the apartment. If there's any magic besides yours, Naveed's and the Kinjos, we'll find our thief," Baz said.

"My magic?" Alice whispered. As Alice imagined all the ways a magic trace could go wrong, Hex pleaded with her eyes for her to stay silent. What really worried Alice was Baz picking up on the fact that Alice had used no magic herself to protect the bag. Worse yet, he might discover that the Kinjo's did not have any magic in the apartment because they were not mages either.

Before Alice could think of a reasonable excuse for him not to perform an M-trace, Hex transformed. Now in her jinn form, she could speak. "I will examine the magic myself," she said.

Baz and Alice both sat stunned in silence, Alice full of gratitude and Baz in bewilderment. "This must be serious for you to change form in front of...well, I suppose you have shown Alice your true form before," Baz said. There was something in his eyes as he looked at Alice. She wanted to imagine it was awe, maybe even attraction, but it was likely surprise that Hex had shown herself to a mage other than himself.

"I will perform the m-trace," Hex repeated.

Baz raised an eyebrow. "May I ask why you're volunteering?"

Hex looked at Naveed. Still in his cat-jinn form, Naveed looked between Hex and Alice, then settled his eyes on Baz. Baz sighed.

"I know you're a jinn. I fought alongside you, remember?" Baz said.

Naveed transformed. He seemed to have made himself a foot taller than usual in his blue, burly form. Crossing his arms made his muscles bulge as he towered over Baz.

"You would not be able to comprehend any magic that could break my seal. It would take more than a human's feeble talent," Naveed said.

Baz showed no sign of intimidation under Naveed's stare. "You're saying only a jinn could break your magic?"

"You underestimate humans," Hex said.

"You underestimate me," Baz said. He waved a hand as if dismissing Naveed's argument, "I can trace jinn magic as well as any other type – right down to the source."

In a soft voice, Hex said, "You have your uncle's affairs to handle."

Baz regarded Hex silently, studying her face as if he could mine it for secrets. After a long while, he stood. "All right," Baz said.

Alice rose from the chair and walked with Baz back to the foyer. She was about to thank him when a knock sounded at the door. Baz stiffened.

"If you'll excuse me, I'm afraid I have an unpleasant task ahead."

Alice nodded. That had to be Titania at the door. Though she knew it was wrong, Alice felt her heart flutter as she interpreted his words as a break-up. "I understand," Alice said as she began walking to the door.

"Alice," Baz called her back. His eyes darted between

Alice and the door in uncharacteristic uncertainty. "If you could part ways here, I'd appreciate it. Titania tends to misinterpret situations." Baz said.

Alice blinked a few times. Misinterpret? Did he mean that Titania would imagine Alice and Baz were…intimate? Swallowing, Alice realized that word had gone around about her outburst in Readings & Co., and Alice imagined the gossip was that she had feelings for Baz. Turning her head so Baz wouldn't see her blush, Alice looked at Naveed.

Naveed stepped forward and grabbed at Alice's arm. "Please allow me," He said, letting the sarcasm sneak into his tone. Alice frowned, nearly tripping as he tugged. Did he have to make it so apparent that she couldn't use magic to make an exit?

In a far more delicate fashion, Hex lifted a hand to Naveed's forward. He immediately relaxed his grip on Alice and gave Hex his attention. Hex slid her arm around his elbow. It may have been Alice's imagination, but a shiver seemed to run through Naveed's body at her touch.

"You may escort us both," Hex said.

Naveed said nothing, he just kept his eyes on Hex as they began to fade from sight. Alice knew it would make her dizzy, but she turned her head toward Baz, uttering goodbye as she disappeared along with the two jinn.

When the world came into view again, Alice was in Mrs. Kinjo's kitchen. For the first time since traveling via Naveed's magic, Alice did not feel sick. She wasn't even the slightest bit dizzy. She narrowed her eyes at Naveed as he dropped her arm. He reached to clasp Hex's hand, but she slid her arm out of his within seconds.

"Where did you store the bag?" Hex asked.

Naveed's lips dipped as he replied. "In the upper cabinet above the fridge." He pointed.

As Hex reached for it, Alice jabbed the back of her hand into Naveed's ribs. "Ow," he whispered, though it couldn't have actually hurt.

"That's for using your magic like a spinning teacup ride every time you took me anywhere," Alice accused.

"Not my fault, you were always in a hurry," Naveed replied.

She could've launched into a rant, he knew he was making her sick the way he traveled so fast from one place to another, he just didn't care. Before Alice could argue, a bright gold light caught Alice's and Naveed's attention. Hex, floating so that her head and arms were above the fridge, had her hands in the open cabinet. The glow emanating from them radiated so brightly, Alice lifted a hand to shield her eyes. When the golden hue faded, Hex removed her hands, the cabinet doors swung shut, and she turned around.

Lowering herself gracefully to the ground, Hex said, "We must get the wand back immediately."

"Why? What did you find?" Naveed asked.

"Was it jinn magic – I mean, someone other than you and Naveed?" Alice asked.

"Worse. A jinn eater, a warlock– someone strong enough to be a threat to all of the magic world," Hex said.

"Only a level ten wizard would have that kind of magic," Naveed said. For the first time since Alice had met him, Naveed looked genuinely afraid.

"Another level ten? I thought there was only Rhys Merlin now," Alice said.

Hex walked past Alice, not looking at her as she replied, "There's also O'Crowly."

Alice shook her head, puzzled. "Doesn't it makes sense that O'Crowly's magic was on the cabinet? The items Naveed put in there were O'Crowly's."

"Alice has a point. If another mage or jinn broke my magic, their spells might have been overshadowed by the magic infused in O'Crowly's possession. It's reactive – even to my magic," Naveed said.

"And what about this?" Hex said, finally turned to look at Alice and Naveed. She was pointing at the little table in the corner of the kitchen. The bonsai had been full of leaves yesterday. Wilting as they were, they were still green. Now, however, the tree was bare, and the fallen leaves below the thin branches were dry and black.

"How did this happen?" Alice walked forward, embracing the dead plant. It was dry and felt like sandpaper in the places that didn't feel like crumbly charcoal.

"Bonsai are sensitive to magic. Even the dismal energies of the untalented can affect the plant and vice versa."

"A powerful warlock used his magic in this room," Naveed said, his hands forming into fists.

"But it's not necessarily O'Crowly, right? Rhys defeated him," Alice said.

"It may not be the same O'Crowly, but it's the same bloodline. Perhaps he was not the last of the first warlock's descendants."

"So there's a descendant of Arthur O'Crowly in Urbana? What does he want with O'Crowly's wand?" Alice said, worried she might not want to find out the answer.

Hex lifted her chin as if finding new resolve, "There is only one thing a warlock like O'Crowly wants: power." Hex looked at Naveed. "But there are two of us and many powerful mages in Urbana."

"Yeah, not that I'm not confident, but there's just the little problem: We don't know what O'Crowly looks like. He could be going by any name. If he's a descendent, none of us know what he looks like, he could be any-"

The door creaked open. Alice felt her heart stop as she turned around. Mrs. Kinjo raised an eyebrow as she peeked into the doorway.

"Alice?"

"Um…yes?" Alice said as if it was normal for her to walk into Mrs. Kinjo's apartment uninvited. But Mrs. Kinjo didn't comment about her break-in. Instead, she stuck her cane forward and walked into the kitchen as if nothing were wrong. One foot inside, she stopped and pointed her cane past Alice.

"Who is your new friend?" Mrs. Kinjo asked.

Alice turned her eyes to look at Hex, but instead of a gold-skinned jinn, Hex had assumed her cat-jinn form. Naveed likewise was a black cat again. Mrs. Kinjo didn't wait for her to explain anything about the additional cat.

"Oh, kurimaya, the black cat who roams this street. Yes, I know you," Mrs. Kinjo lowered herself into a kitchen chair and reached down to the floor. Hex into her reach and leaned into Mrs. Kinjo's soft hands.

"I…I brought her inside, thinking she might be hungry. I didn't think you'd mind." Alice said. She shrugged when Naveed and Hex both looked at her questioningly. It was the first excuse she could think of for being in the Kinjo's kitchen.

"Mind? Of course not." Mrs. Kinjo pointed to the cabinets. "I had Eric buy cat food for Fluffy. It's in the upper left there."

"That sounds great," Alice said, throwing a wincing smile toward Hex. Alice hoped Hex wouldn't be insulted by the idea of eating feline foods. But Hex looked unperturbed. Naveed was the one sticking out his tongue in a look that even on a cat translated to repulsion. Alice walked to the cabinet, took out the can of Kitty Cuisine, and rummaged through the drawers for a can opener.

"The second drawer," Mrs. Kinjo instructed.

As Alice searched, she asked, "So, has anyone come up here today?"

"Mr. Coulson came in to say hello," Mrs. Kinjo reminded Alice. She was more interested in whether the customer who'd asked about wands had wandered upstairs. But, Mrs. Kinjo went on about Mr. Coulson. "Such a kind soul. He asked about why you don't want to work at the museum."

"Hamee," Alice began, addressing Mrs. Kinjo by the Okinawan word for grandmother.

Mrs. Kinjo put her hands up. "Not my business, I know. But he values your knowledge. No other graduate knows what you know about rare and antique artifacts."

A sideways half-smile snaked into Alice's lips. "What I learned from you, you mean," Alice said, as she opened the can of tuna.

Mrs. Kinjo shrugged her shoulders. "I know only what I learned from my husband, and most people don't believe the things he saw in his travels."

Alice plopped the tuna into a bowl and set it down in front of Hex, who turned her head away. She was still enjoying Mrs. Kinjo stroking her back in a gentle massage. Naveed sat opposite Hex and stared at her, which would have creeped Alice out if she were Hex. Alice couldn't help but grimace as Naveed plunged his full-face into the tuna.

As she threw the now-empty cat-food can away, she continued her conversation with Mrs. Kinjo. "It's probably best he didn't believe you since we're supposed to be keeping magic and jinn and all of that secret now."

Hex meowed as Mrs. Kinjo's fingers lifted from her fur. Naveed looked up from the bowl, tuna dripping off his whiskers. Mrs. Kinjo brought a hand to her lips. "Were we supposed to keep that secret? I thought we were not telling the witches about us not having magic?"

Alice sank into the chair. "That's true. But we can't tell the un-, the non-magical people, about the witches either. Hamee, you didn't tell Mr. Coulson about Magic Row, did you?"

Mrs. Kinjo dropped her hand, waving it at the same time. "I don't think he believed me. Magic is as real to rational people as love is to a cynic, not at all. No one ever believes my stories – except for you, Alice."

Alice tried to take the compliment. If she was honest, she was a cynic. Or had been her whole – no, not her whole life. She'd had a childhood optimism once, hadn't she? *What had happened?* She thought. *Oh, that's right: A fire burned it up.* The image of her mother trapped in a house in flames came to mind, which was pure imagination since she hadn't actually seen her mother's death. The social worker had never even let her see the body.

Swallowing the lump in her throat, Alice managed to smile. "I'm sure it's fine," she said, referring to Mr. Coulson back in the present moment.

Mrs. Kinjo rose, the chair creaking as she did, causing Hex to jump to her feet. Naveed perked his head up from the bowl, looking around to see what happened. His tuna soaked whiskers sagged. Attempting to clean himself off, Naveed shook his head. Hex pulled back, drooping her lip in disgust as tuna flew everywhere.

"Stop that," Alice whispered.

Mrs. Kinjo had made it to the bonsai. She put a hand on one empty branch. Alice stood and walked over, raising a hand to Mrs. Kinjo's shoulder to console her.

"My thumb is not as green as I hoped," Mrs. Kinjo said.

"How…when did this happen?" Alice asked.

"I'm not sure. Mr. Coulson noticed it when we came in here for tea." Mrs. Kinjo turned to Alice, whose mix of concern and regret showed on her face. "I don't blame you. I'm sure it wasn't the soil," Mrs. Kinjo said, tapping Alice's face gently.

The soil? Alice hadn't even thought of that. Could Mr. Gowdie have had some effect on the bonsai? Gowdie wouldn't have much business if he sold products that sabotaged his customers. Then again, he seemed evil enough to be a warlock.

Alice walked to the table with the bonsai and picked up the soil bag. "I'll look into it," Alice said. She never liked confrontations, but she'd be more than happy to get her money back from a swindler like Gowdie.

"Don't go to too much trouble." Mrs. Kinjo said, walk past Alice to the door. She stopped abruptly and turned around. "I almost forgot: A woman came in asking for you, the one who was here about your necklace last week."

Alice touched her ruby-red charmed stone. "Belinda?" she asked.

"Names escape me. The woman said she found something in the photos of the party. At least, I think that is what she said; I'm not sure I understood correctly."

"It's all right. I know what she means. I'll clean up and go see her." Alice said, walking over to the tuna bowl and the mess Naveed had made.

"You'll have to see her tomorrow. She said something about preparing for a date tonight. She asked if you'd go to her apartment tomorrow at lunch." As Mrs. Kinjo left the kitchen, Hex and Naveed transformed. Hex began to fade. Naveed took hold of her hand before she could disappear.

Hex turned her head sharply, her gold eyes glowing anger. "I must go," Hex said.

"Without a good-bye?" Naveed smiled…seductively? Alice didn't think his baring his sharp fangs said "playful" as much as "threatening," but Hex didn't seem scared.

She yanked her hand away. "I must warn Baz about O'Crowly as soon as possible," she said, fading from view as she spoke.

"She's deliberately ignoring me." Naveed frowned.

"She needs space," Alice said.

"She's causing needless pain for us both. We were meant to be together," Naveed said, with all too much passion.

"That," Alice pointed at Naveed. "That needs to stop. You're getting obsessive," Alice said as she walked closer.

Naveed's eyes widened. He looked away, crossing his arms and puffing out his chest. "I am a jinn in love."

"What I just saw- that wasn't love," Alice said.

Naveed breathed deep, his chest expanding like his heart needed the space. "I am a fire jinn. My love is an all-consuming flame."

"Not love," Alice repeated.

"How would you know?" Naveed snapped—literally, he snapped his fingers, and a flame danced over his thumb.

Alice smacked both hands around Naveed's fist, smothering the fire between her fingers. He pulled back, eyes wide and mouth open. Alice let go and smirked, thoroughly enjoying his shock.

Naveed scratched his head. "Are you sure you're not a fire jinn, too? Make you angry enough, and your fire comes out."

"So don't make me angry," Alice said.

"How did I make you angry? I simply pointed out that you've never…" Naveed trailed off as he saw the anger in her eyes.

Alice may not have ever been in love, but Naveed was

wrong to imply she didn't know what love felt like. Some-where, buried by years of pain, Alice had a memory of a mother who'd love her. Alice ignored the sting of love lost, still burning a hole in her chest. She picked up the bag of soil and clutched Naveed's arm. "Let's take this back to Gowdie's. And don't make me sick this time," she said. Naveed had no choice but to do as she wished.

FOURTEEN

Malicious Magic

G owdie scowled as he saw Alice walk through the door.

"If you're back to give me another piece of your mind, you can save it," Mr. Gowdie said.

Alice plunked the soil onto the counter, not caring as some rushed out of the bag.

"What's the idea?" Mr. Gowdie said, clicking his fingers. A mini brush and dustpan went to work on the fallen dirt.

Alice pointed. "That soil killed my friend's bonsai." To be fair, Alice didn't know that was true, but she also wouldn't have been surprised if he was conspiring with whoever had broken into the Kinjo's home.

"Impossible," Mr. Gowdie said.

"I have the dead plant to prove it." Alice raised her fingers as if she was going to cast a spell, "Should I fetch it to show you?"

Naveed jumped onto the counter and meowed as if backing up Alice's threat. Gowdie glowered. Then he frowned, moving away from the counter.

"No need. I can test this soil right now," Mr. Gowdie said. He muttered to himself as he walked to the back-room, "Try to come into my store accusing me, by the moon, the nerve of this one." As before, the shelves moved with a wave of Mr. Gowdie's hand, and the red velvet curtains appeared. Mr. Gowdie parted the curtain, closing them quickly behind him as he entered the back room.

While he was gone, Alice looked around the store. There were several bonsai, beautiful and blooming inside a glass cabinet. Alice was tempted to purchase the one with tiny pink flowers, but she wouldn't give Mr. Gowdie the satisfaction of more business. She was here to recoup her money. That was it.

Still, they were beautiful. Alice reached toward the glass, hoping to open it for a closer look. Mr. Gowdie came back with a mini-briefcase in his hand.

"What are you doing? Trying to steal from me?"

"What? Of course not," Alice said.

"Don't bother. I put the spell on it myself and rein-forced it with several incantations. I doubt even a ninth level could get in there."

"I was just looking," Alice said through her teeth. It was a good thing she didn't have magic, or Alice might have pranked hexed him already. Naveed meowed as if in response to her just thinking about it. She did not make it a wish.

"Those are far out of your price range, anyway," Mr. Gowdie said.

"Why, do you charge extra for defective products?" Alice's foul mood was seeping into her comebacks. She needed to get a hold of her anger. Only, as she walked back to the counter, she realized it wasn't anger. Sure, she was annoyed with her argument with Naveed. But they bickered all the time.

If the soil wasn't defective, the dead bonsai was just more proof that Hex was right. There was a high-level warlock in Urbana giving off vibes of pure evil. And if it wasn't Mr. Gowdie, Alice had no idea of the warlock's identity. Alice shuddered at the thought.

She folded her arms, leaning on the counter as she watched Mr. Gowdie open his little briefcase. The case was lined with vials of powders and liquids. Mr. Gowdie picked up a bottle and tapped it with his index finger.

"What is all that?" Alice asked.

"Testers. This one will tell me if the balance of magic is right for the soil. Green is a perfect balance," he said as he snapped on a glove. He spread a pinch of powder over the dustpan.

The powder shot up in a *poof* of green dust and dissipated into the air. Mr. Gowdie smiled— vindicated. Alice frowned.

"But…it can't be…" Alice said.

"Oh, don't be too hard on yourself, Miss Adelcraft. Bonsai are sensitive to magic

"That explains why you don't have any in your shop," Alice said.

Mr. Gowdie's smile faded. "Oh, look at that." Mr. Gowdie held up his wristwatch, "5pm. We're closed. Have a good day, Miss Adelcraft."

Alice clutched the bag tight, spilling dust along the way— not entirely accidentally— as she walked to the door. She and Naveed walked down the street, passing A Witch's Thrift Shop, where Celeste was closing up for the day. She tapped her wrist and called out to Hazel or Vestra to hurry up so she could leave.

"You can do that tomorrow. Time to go," Celeste said, then she turned and noticed Alice and the direction from which she was coming. Celeste crossed her arms. "Don't tell me you're still investigating?"

Alice held up the bag of soil and pointed back toward The Essential Mage. "Just trying to make a return," Alice said.

Celeste laughed. "To Gowdie? That old stickler won't give you anything."

"Why do people shop there?" Alice asked.

"He has some of the best tools for the Talented in Urbana."

"At prices no one can afford," Alice said.

Celeste grinned. "That's why they come to me. Speaking of which, you haven't come into A Witch's Thrift Shop since you found out about Baz's uncle's murder."

"I've been busy," Alice said. She didn't want to admit that she'd been involved with Perseus' will reading. Alice had been avoiding Celeste since she'd disregarded her advice about staying away from Baz.

"Busy with what?" Celeste said, her eyebrow issuing a challenge.

"Nothing," Alice said, avoiding the lecture she knew Celeste would give.

"All right. Then if you're not busy, why not join me for a night out? Vestra's dragging me along with her and her friends for ladies night at some bar and grill restaurant. Not really my thing, but she insists that if I don't go, I'll end up a shriveled-up, lonely old maid." Alice raised an eyebrow, not following the logic. Celeste shook her head, "Don't ask. Let's just say Vestra insisted that there will be loads of single, se…sensational sights." Celeste swapped the adjective out as Hazel walked outside.

"Aren't Vestra and Eric–"

"They're still going strong. As a matter of fact, Vestra

invited me to a star shower tomorrow night. She seems to think I don't have a life of my own lately," Celeste said.

"Oh, weird," Alice vaguely remembered having made a comment to that effect.

"What's weird?" Hazel asked.

"Vestra. But what's new? So are you coming tonight?" Celeste asked.

"Tonight? Mom said you're joining us for dinner?" Hazel looked at Alice expectantly.

"Oh, I almost forgot. That was at Ambrosia at seven, right?" Alice pointed across the street at the restaurant across from The Essential Mage.

"That's right," Hazel beamed.

"I'll see you then." Alice returned Hazel's smile and shrugged at Celeste, "I guess you're on your own with all those...sensational sights," Alice said.

Celeste frowned. "I didn't ask to go, you know. Maybe I should cancel."

"No, go. Vestra won't let you hear the end of it if you don't," Alice said.

"You don't have to go somewhere if you don't want to – it's not like you're thirteen and have to listen to your parents." Hazel shrugged.

"So true. It's not like you're thirteen, Celeste," Alice repeated, chuckling. It was good to be around friends who knew nothing of missing wands and warlocks in town. Alice's feeling of impending doom was lifting.

Celeste scowled. "Yes, well, I'm also not Vestra's age."

"I'm sure no one will notice anything but your incredible figure tonight," Alice said.

"Yes, well, they'd better not, but I think I'll spell my dress to give the illusion of an hourglass figure– just to be sure. See you tomorrow," she said, smiling as she walked toward the bus stop.

Hazel waved good-bye, then bent down to pet Naveed. Alice noticed her sad expression and knelt next to her. "What's wrong, Hazel? You don't want to go to Ambrosia tonight?"

Hazel shook her head. "It's not that. Dad wants us to move out of Merlin's Shadow."

Alice's half-smile disappeared. "I heard about that. It's probably best, though, with your dad being..." Alice didn't finish the sentence.

Hazel caught the drift. "Everyone here thinks he's just like everyone else, though. Nobody really knows, except you and Celeste. I don't see why we have to go."

She stood up, and so did Alice. Together, they crossed the street. As they walked, Alice said, "It's not easy fitting in somewhere when you're different." She spoke from experience, and not just because she was Untalented. "People need to be free to be themselves. It's really the only way to be happy." Alice almost felt like she was talking to herself. She couldn't really be happy with someone like Baz, even if he did feel something around her. He'd never accept her true self.

"People should be able to be themselves anywhere, with anyone," Hazel said.

That was true, too. But the world wasn't like that - not yet, anyway. On the other side of the street, Alice and Hazel stopped. Alice put a hand on Hazel's shoulder. "Look, you don't know what your parents will decide. I'm sure whatever decision they make, it'll be for your own best interest. They love you and Zade."

"And we love Magic Row, and Merlin's Shadow, and... everyone here," Hazel argued.

"I know," Alice said softly. "I wish you could stay, too, but-"

"Good. Then you can convince my parents tonight," Hazel said.

She turned around faster than Alice could get another word out. Alice felt played. She looked down at Naveed, who was only shaking his head, his little cat ears waggling at what he'd just heard.

"Not a word," Alice said, as she and Naveed disappeared to go home.

FIFTEEN

An Evening of Eavesdropping

I t took an hour for Alice to dress up, another half hour to do make-up, and an eon to wrestle her hair with the straightener. It wasn't doing any good. It was a bad hair night, and nothing was going to change that. With the clock at two minutes to seven, Alice gave up and called it done. She walked out to see Naveed dozing on the sofa.

"Ahem," Alice interrupted his snores.

Naveed opened one eye, then two, and blinked himself awake. He stretched as he rose from the sofa. Then he transformed into his cat form.

"You're not going to say anything?" Alice asked, holding her dress in a half-curtsy style.

Naveed turned back into a jinn. "It took you long enough," he said. Then he transformed again.

Alice walked to the door, grabbing her fancier night-out purse. "You're impossible," she said as she transferred the essentials from her day-bag into it.

Naveed transformed again. "You take two hours to get ready, and *I'm* impossible?"

"Let's just go," Alice said.

"You're not going to cry, are you?"

"What? No," Alice shot him her best *"you're insane"* look.

"Good, because girls do that way too-"

"I'm not going to cry," Alice snapped. She fiddled with the frizzy loose bun self-consciously. "It just would have been nice to be complimented before going out."

"Complimented?" Naveed looked like he needed a dictionary.

"You know, a *'you look nice'* or something."

"But you always look nice," Naveed said. Alice smiled. "What?" Naveed asked, genuine confusion spreading across his face.

Alice put a hand on Naveed's shoulder–or tried to, he was too tall for her to reach. "Nothing. Let's go," Alice said, gently this time.

"Women." Naveed rolled his eyes as he transformed into his black cat-jinn form and pressed against Alice's ankle. She found herself outside Ambrosia restaurant in the chilly night air.

As Alice opened the door and walked inside, she noticed a man standing close enough to feel the warmth radiating off his skin. What's more, Alice did not see Naveed at her feet. She moved left and right, looking down when the man tapped on Alice's shoulder.

"Alice," Naveed said in his voice. He was standing in the front in his jinn form, big and blue and everything. Thank goodness the restaurant curved to the side, so no one was shocked by a seven-foot being.

"What are you doing?" Alice whispered.

"Don't blame me. Qadira never brought me to places like this. They must have a spell on the restaurant. It took me by surprise, but I'm sure I can outdo the magic." Naveed raised a hand.

Alice grabbed his elbow. "No, don't. Someone might have already seen you." He couldn't become a black cat again now, or they'd know "Fluffy McScratchins" wasn't just Alice's familiar. "You'll just have to go with it tonight. Could you make yourself human?" Naveed shrunk to a generous 6foot height. "Your skin is still blue." Alice whispered.

"You want me to change my color to be more presentable?" He raised an offended eyebrow.

"Blue isn't a human color," Alice said as she saw a waitress rounding the corner.

Naveed's eyebrow went higher. "Actually, there have been a few cases in human history of—"

"Naveed, I wish you would make yourself look human right now," Alice said.

Confined to the wish, Naveed stopped arguing. "Do you have a specific color in mind?" he asked.

Alice face-palmed. "Could you please give me a break?" she asked as the waitress noticed them and grabbed two menus.

Naveed's skin took on a subtle change, now like that of a dark brown man. It was close enough to the original blue in the restaurant lighting that the hostess may not have noticed. Alice let out a relieved breath.

"Thank you," Alice said.

The hostess approached, asking, "Table for two?"

"Actually, we're with the Willows. I think the reservation might be under-"

Naveed stepped in front of Alice. "Is that a Nabataean jinn block?" he asked, pointing to a stone block carved with four columns running up each side.

"Yeah, it's a re-creation of the ones in Petra. They were a gift to the owner," the hostess said as she used her magic to flip through something like Rolodex to find their reservation.

"They're used to keep jinn from blending in," Naveed explained to Alice.

"You know your history. I'm impressed," the hostess said, done with her search.

"Why do you have this?" Alice asked.

"The owner is superstitious. She put all sorts of wards up everywhere," the waitress said. Alice had recently learned from Celeste that wards were items placed in homes and other buildings to keep evil away.

"But why a ward against jinn? They aren't evil as far as I know," Alice asked.

The waitress shrugged. "I just work here, I don't know. I guess it's a good thing we don't have any in Urbana, right?" She laughed, not knowing how close she was to being hexed or whatever was the jinn equivalent. "Ah, here we go, Willows," the waitress said.

Alice put a hand on Naveed's arm. His hand had already curled into a fist as they followed the waitress to the table. Naveed eventually relaxed, and Alice let go. She did look up at him, concerned about how the effect the ward might have on him.

Before she could ask if they should leave, Naveed bent to whisper into Alice's ear, "That statue this one is one-tenth the size of the original. It wouldn't be effective against a jinn of any real power."

It explained why Naveed was able to counter the spell. He looked human enough, though perhaps a bit taller than a normal man. Though as for that, Alice spied Ron at the bar picking up a take-out bag. He smiled and nodded as he saw Alice. His grin faded as Alice reached her destination. Alice looked past the plum, satin tablecloth of the long rectangular table to the happy family seated opposite them.

In the royal, purple booth, Liza and her family sat smiling, all dressed for a night out and looking fabulous. Liza's floral v-shaped dress showed off her figure, usually hidden under loose blouses and palazzo pants. Her blonde hair was pulled back on one side with a butterfly clip. Alice glanced back at Ron. As if sensing her eyes, Ron blinked and broke his open-mouth stare at Liza. He met Alice's sympathetic frown with a forced smile and turned quickly toward the front door.

"Alice, I didn't know you were bringing a guest," Liza said, pulling her attention back to the table.

Tom stood and held out a hand to Naveed. Naveed stared at the open palm like it was the first time a human had ever extended such a greeting. Alice gave Naveed a light jab in the side before he took the gesture. Tom winced as they shook. Alice cleared her throat, and Naveed took the cue to let go.

"That's…quite a grip you've got," Tom said, massaging his now-free hand.

"I'm sorry if I hurt you," Naveed said, his smile saying otherwise.

"No, no, of course not, I'm fine," Tom said.

Tom reached toward a chair for Alice and out it slid before he could touch it. Surprised by the display of magic, Tom looked at his family. Zade's mischievous grin gave him away. Alice winked as she sat down. Naveed flicked his hand and pushed the chair in with his magic before Tom could make any other pretend gentlemanly gesture. Tom smiled awkwardly and sat down.

"So, who is your mystery man?" Hazel asked.

"Have I seen you before?" Zade asked, looking Naveed up and down.

"No," Naveed said forcefully.

"He's…well, it's a funny thing, see I wasn't expecting

him either…he just kind of popped into town…" Alice said, floundering for an explanation.

"That doesn't really answer the question," Zade said.

"He's…" Alice looked at Naveed. Could she get away with it? He had made his skin a few shades darker than hers, but he could pass as related to Alice. Couldn't he?

Naveed put an arm around Alice, "She is my…"

Oh no, what was he going to say? Master? Lover? Alice almost gagged at the thought. Almost as a reflex, she blurted out the answer, "Sister. I'm his sister. Yep, this is my brother."

Naveed looked sick. If anything, he turned a shade lighter right in front of their eyes. Alice had to step on his foot to get him to stop changing, which he did.

"You have a brother?" Zade asked.

"I don't remember you mentioning him," Hazel added.

"I'm sure Alice has a good reason for that," Tom said, almost challenging her with his eyes.

"That's because I'm not really her brother," Naveed said, letting go of her shoulder.

Alice winced. "He's a half-brother. He's from Egypt, so we really didn't know each other growing up. But he's in town for a while, so we're catching up." The words were tumbling out of Alice before she could stop herself. She picked up her glass of water and drank quickly to keep from rambling.

"How fascinating," Tom said.

"What was your name?" Liza asked.

"Naveed," he replied.

"Where in Egypt are you from?" Tom inquired.

Naveed caught Alice's eyes, and she silently pleaded for him to go along with her. "Actually, her – our– mother is from Egypt. My father is Jordanian. That is where I grew up." Naveed said, allowing his accent to grow to what it must have been before he came to the USA.

Hazel and Zade launched into a plethora of questions about the area. Alice was fascinated to learn about the ancient city of Petra, with its pink, sandstone cliffs and the jinn who lived in the mountains.

"You know a lot about Jinn," Tom said.

"They are legendary where I'm from," Naveed said.

"Why legend? Aren't they still around?" Zade asked.

Alice held her breath, chewing on her breadstick like it was her last meal. If this conversation went wrong, it might just be the end of her. She gave Naveed a warning glance, but he wasn't looking.

"In Jordan, the jinn-human wars a hundred years ago left very few alive. The jinn of the air fled to other places, and the fire jinn were pushed deeper into the mountain. They hide from humans now," Naveed said.

"Why were they fighting?" Hazel asked.

"Jinn were more powerful than wizards, so naturally, wizards feared them."

"If they were so strong why did they lose? Sounds like the wizards kicked their—"

"Zade," Liza warned.

"Butts," Zade muttered under his breath.

Naveed took a long breath and leaned back in his chair. "Jinn are spirits, so they need a link to the earth to stay alive. The air jinn can link with almost anything, from the air, to water and trees. They do best with crystals and jewels. Fire jinn need sturdier materials— like the earth itself, mountains, and such."

"And gold," Zade said, adding, "Like the oil lamps."

"Those are popular for keeping genies. I mean, we have some lamps in A Witch's Thrift Shop, customers sometimes ask if there are jinn in them, but we don't have any," Hazel rambled. Everyone seemed more interested in Naveed, glancing between him and Hazel as they waited for her to finish. Noticing Zade's eye-roll, Hazel put her head down and kept eating.

Naveed continued with his story. "Wizards used this connection as a way of trapping several jinn inside items like lamps and jewels. Others just had their connection broken completely. No one knows what happened to them. Some say they wander the world, never touching the living, never being seen, except out of the corner of your eye, or in the shadows," Naveed said.

"Shadow people," Alice remembered hearing stories of something similar as a child. She couldn't remember.

"What did the jinn do to the wizards?" Hazel asked.

Naveed stiffened. "They killed them, I suppose."

"No one probably knows because no one goes into the mountains, right?" Zade asked.

Naveed nodded. "The worst part of war is that families have no way to know for sure what happened to loved ones caught by the other side," Naveed said.

"I can't even imagine–" Alice said.

"You can't," Naveed said.

Hazel shivered. Zade starting making ghostly "oohs" and waving his hands.

"Stop it." Hazel swatted his flailing, zombie-like arms away.

"Maybe we could leave the talk about jinn out of the conversation. The owner here isn't partial to them," Liza said.

Naveed's eyebrows lowered like clouds darkening over his expression. "Why-" he began.

"What's everyone ordering?" Alice put a hand on Naveed's arm and glanced sideways at him. He gave her a smile that bared his teeth. Alice silently wondered if his canines had always been that sharp.

They put in their orders with the waitress. Zade tried to get a dessert with his meal, but his mother put an end to that. He pouted as he handed back the menu.

"Stop making a scene," Hazel said.

"Stop making a scene," Zade repeated her words in a mock voice.

Liza looked at Tom, who pulled out his phone, distracted by the sound of a text alert. Turning to the teens, Liza said, "Children, please." She glanced at Tom's phone, but he had it turned away from her.

Hazel straightened her back. "We're young adults, mother." She looked at her brother, adding, "Well, one of us is, anyway."

"Will you cut out all this young adult stuff? You're only doing that because you like Puck, and he isn't even here," Zade said.

Hazel turned cherry red.

"Who's Puck?" Tom asked. His cell phone rang the next second. He held a finger up and rose from the table. "Hello?" Tom answered as he walked toward the hallway in the back of the restaurant.

Liza caught Alice's eye and gave a half-hearted smile.

"He always does that," Zade said, resting his chin in one hand. His mother gave him a tap to remind him no elbows were allowed on the table.

"He's just working," Hazel said, taking a sip of water.

"Your father is trying to build a good life for us," Liza said.

"Yeah, after destroying it," Zade replied, adding, "I'm not even hungry."

"We built a good life here," Hazel said. She looked at Alice for help.

"Maybe there's a compromise. There are some great apartments in Urbana that are not too far away from Merlin's Shadow."

"We haven't decided anything yet," Liza said.

"Dad said we have to move out of town," Zade replied.

"We haven't made definite plans," Liza said. Now she was pleading with her eyes for Alice's assistance. Surprisingly, the help came from Naveed.

"You are lucky to have a second chance. I lost my father young, and a younger sister and older brother, too. But I had no chance to have them back," Naveed said.

"Did they die in the jinn wars?" Zade asked.

"Stupid. Think about it. He'd be, like, hundreds of years old if that was true," Hazel said.

"He could be a level ten wizard for all we know," Zade shot back.

"Even they don't live that long," Hazel said, rolling her eyes.

"Maybe he's a jinn. Did you ever think of that?"

Alice practically inhaled her bite of breadstick. Coughing, she reached for her water. Conversation stopped. Naveed waved the glass to her, and she drank in heaping gulps until the bread dislodged in her throat.

"So how did your dad and siblings die? Ow, why'd you kick me?" Zade asked.

Hazel rolled her eyes.

"I never said they were dead," Naveed answered, "I have no way to know that. Only that my sister was young and loved chasing butterflies. We rarely went to the fields atop the jinn mountains, but my parents thought the fresh air did us good, even though the area was…not always safe for us. My sister wandered off. My father and brother went to look for her, and none of them ever came back."

"Strange. Was it an accident…a cave in or something?" Liza asked.

"Maybe the jinn got them," Zade said.

Hazel buried her head into her hand.

"Zade, maybe we should change the subject," Liza said.

Alice tried to agree, but all that came out was more coughing.

"Are you all right?" Liza asked.

Alice nodded. "I'm just going to go to the restroom. You guys talk," she said, "Talk about something else," she whispered to Naveed as she left the table. On her way to the restroom, Alice passed Tom. He turned away from her. Alice slowed her pace until she made it to the restroom door, then hesitated, listening.

"I've got it all planned. Relax. I'll see you tomorrow." He clicked off the phone and looked left and right.

Alice went into the restroom before he could see her. At the sink, she coughed a few times, gargled some water and spit, trying to get the ache out of her throat. When she was done, Alice looked herself over in the mirror. To her surprise, her hair had a shine to it. The curls were fine, not frizzed, and the loose bun made a perfect loop from the side view. She looked better than she ever had before.

The bathroom door opened. Liza walked to the sink next to Alice and looked into the mirror. She adjusted her hair, nervously fidgeting with her blond strands.

She smiled at Alice. "Sorry, the kids are being so-"

"They're fine," Alice said.

"Are you OK?" Liza asked.

"Yeah, are you?" Alice asked. Liza seemed as distressed as this morning.

"It's not weird, right? Everyone answers their phone at

dinner sometimes. And so what if it's a woman, she's his assistant and…" Liza abandoned the sentence.

"You think he's cheating?" Alice asked.

Liza's eyes widened, "What? No, I…" her eyes teared. She shook her head and waved a paper towel over to her. Dabbing her eyes, she said, "We were separated for three years. It would be natural if he grew close to another woman."

"He's on the phone that often?"

"Every night. He's always answering his calls and keeping it secret from me. If I ask him about it, he gets so angry."

She struggled to fight back the tears. Alice pulled her into a hug. She wasn't good at knowing what to say, so she waited for Liza to speak again.

Liza pulled away. "It's silly. I'm just being paranoid, right?" she said.

"It's not silly. Maybe you should talk to Tom, tell him how you feel, you know, confront him," Alice said. She wanted to tell her right then about Titania. After all, Baz knew. Liza had a right to know too. "There's something you should know," she began. Another woman walked into the restroom. Alice paused. It was one thing to tell Liza about Tom and Titania. It was another to fuel gossip around Magic Row. Baz, ever a gentleman, hadn't wanted rumors about Titania to spread. But he might be able to show Liza the pictures, it might hurt less coming from someone who knew her pain. Alice looked into Liza's teary blue eyes. "Listen, Tom's on the Delvaux case, and Baz has a way of finding things out, maybe if he-"

"Oh no, don't do that. I'm sure it's nothing. Tom has been busy. Like you said, he's on a high profile case," Liza dried her eyes and attempted a smile.

"Liza," Alice said, trying to talk reason into her with her tone.

"Come on, before dinner gets cold," Liza said, walking out of the restroom.

Alice followed, even though she wasn't hungry. Back at the table, Tom stood to help Liza back into her chair. Naveed just looked at Alice.

"What?" He asked, oblivious to gentlemanly gestures.

Alice pulled out her own chair and sat down. Tom's phone on the table vibrated. Reading the screen upside down, Alice made out Client 01 before Tom grabbed the phone quickly.

"Pardon me," Tom said. He walked away from the table again.

Liza looked at Alice, who gave her a reassuring smile. The kids continued their conversation about Jordan and magic in the Middle East. Alice added in a few tidbits about Egypt wherever she could, while Liza kept glancing at Tom.

His food was cold by the time he returned to the table. Liza put her hands on the bottom of his plate and warmed it with her magic as Tom apologized. "Work," he explained.

"Must be important. Your #1 client, maybe?" Alice challenged Tom with her eyes.

He stared at her as he folded his napkin and reset it on his lap. "He was my very first client, yes, and when he contacted me again, well, it's just an easy way for me to keep track of who is calling. But all my clients are a priority. Incidentally, Alice, the firm has a client who is interested in the objects in your care from Perseus' safe."

Alice looked at Naveed and back at Tom, bewildered. "I thought will readings were confidential," Alice said.

"You know how the community is. Someone must have

leaked the information," Tom said, resuming his meal.

"I wonder who in the reading would spread the word," Alice said.

"Well, however he found out about it, he is interested in purchasing the items from you," Tom replied.

"Which items specifically?" Alice asked.

"He doesn't actually know what Merlin had in Perseus' safe, only that if they belonged to Merlin, they must have been items of value. Now that Merlin is gone-"

"Excuse me?" Alice said.

"I mean, now that he's left Urbana, he won't have use for them."

"He's coming back," Alice said.

"Is he? Oh, pardon me. He gave you power of attorney...I just assumed that meant...well, never mind then. I'll pass the good news along to my client," Tom said.

"Who is your client?" Alice asked.

"I'm sorry, I can't tell you that, that information is part of lawyer-client privilege. You understand," Tom said.

"Sure," Alice replied.

The rest of the meal went without incident until dessert arrived when Alice felt Naveed jab her in the side. She jerked her head toward him and whispered, "What?"

He leaned into her ear, saying just one word, "O'Crowly."

Alice froze. Slowly, when she could muster the courage, she looked around the restaurant. She couldn't see or hear anyone out of the ordinary – or what was ordinary for Magic Row. Even when she turned all the way around and looked out the window, she saw no one.

"Is something wrong?" Liza asked.

Alice twisted back to face the table. "No," she tried smiling. "I just realized how late it is. I have to be somewhere soon."

"But we just got dessert," Hazel said.

"The best part of the meal," Zade added, his eyes locked onto the three-layered chocolate pudding pie in front of him.

Alice slid her chair back, "I'm sorry, I'll pay my part at the counter."

"Don't be silly. We invited you, we'll take care of the check," Tom said.

Liza's smile widened. Slipping her arm around her husband's, she said, "I'll see you tomorrow."

"Sure, thanks," Alice nodded and smiled as she rose.

Naveed pushed his chair back and stood, towering over the table. He dropped his napkin onto the chair and turned to leave. Then, he paused and faced the Willows, scratching the back of his head as he thought of what to say.

"Um, thank you for the meal," Naveed said as if showing gratitude was forced labor.

Naveed followed Alice to the door and opened it before she could.

"Thanks," Alice said, impressed that he knew how to be a gentleman. "And thank you for whatever magic you did to make me look, you know, just…thanks," she said.

"I only made you see yourself the way others see you," Naveed said, then he put an arm out in front of her and stopped.

With it dark outside and no one around, Alice whispered to Naveed, "What's wrong?"

Naveed was looking across the street. Mr. Gowdie's light was on, though the store was closed. A shadowy black figure stopped in the window. It faced Alice, lingered, and then dissolved to nothing in plain sight. Alice couldn't tell who it was, but she could clearly make out one thing:

It was a woman.

SIXTEEN

For Love of Money

A lice went to Reading & Co. first thing the next morning. She meant not only to apologize about leaving early and thank Liza for taking care of the dinner, but she wanted to talk with Merlin again. She'd feel a lot better if he were in Urbana while a warlock like O'Crowly was in town.

Reading & Co. was uncharacteristically quiet as Alice entered, despite plenty of customers eating in the café. Alice felt every eye follow her as she walked to the Reading Room. She didn't know why until she saw Baz seated alone by at a table in the back.

She kept her head down, hoping to pass by without him noticing— no such luck.

"Alice," he called out to her.

She walked over, aware of the would-be gossipers watching. Naveed didn't care. He jumped right up onto the chair opposite Baz, his cat-jinn eyes searching Baz's breakfast plate for something good. Considering it was a simple toast and jam, Naveed wasn't likely to find anything he liked.

"Good morning," Alice said.

"I would ask you to join me, but I'm supposed to be meeting Charlotte this morning." Baz looked at his watch. "Seems she's running late."

Alice pointed toward the Reading room. "I'm just here to see Liza."

"I heard your brother is in town? I hadn't realized you had a sibling."

"A half-brother. You actually know him. His name is *Naveed*," Alice said, looking at the cat-jinn resting his head on one paw on the table like a human. As if pretending to be a cat took too much energy, he let out an unconvincing "meow."

Baz's open mouth told her he was at a loss for words.

"We were at Ambrosia's last night," Alice explained.

"Ah, I see," Baz replied, realization forming over his face. He must have known about the anti-jinn policy the owner kept. She'd have to ask him about that later.

"Actually, we saw something…well… I'm not sure what we saw exactly, but there was a woman at Gowdie's last night long after the store was closed. She disappeared the moment we saw her - as if she hadn't wanted us to see her. We thought maybe it was Charlotte," Alice said.

"You're not the first to see a mage go into Gowdie's after closing. Gowdie accommodates some of his clients who can't make regular hours. Or so I've heard."

"You don't think that's strange? I mean, the way she disappeared– it's odd," Alice said.

Baz shrugged. "A little, maybe but-" Baz stopped and looked at the door as another customer entered.

Alice turned around to see Titania. She walked straight over to Baz with a grin plastered across her face. Again she knocked shoulders with Alice and didn't apologize as she stood in Alice's place.

"Baz, I think we need to speak," Titania said.

Baz glanced at Alice before meeting Titania's eyes. "I think I made myself clear yesterday."

Titania's smile grew. "But today is a new day, and I have a feeling you are going to change your mind. Stay right here, I'll get us some coffee."

Baz lifted his cup, "I have mine." He said.

Titania took his cup. "It's empty. I'll get you another."

"Titania," Baz said his tone warning.

"Baz, please. Just have one coffee with me and hear me out. That's all I'm asking," Titania said. She turned, nearly bumping into Alice again. Alice realized she'd been overtly eavesdropping and backed away. But Titania walked directly in Alice's path, whispering as she walked by, "That cat better be out of my seat by the time I get back."

Alice didn't tell her that she was the one being catty. Instead, she shoed Naveed down, walked to the reading room door, and knocked twice. Alice glanced one last time at Baz before the door opened. His eyes met hers with an unreadable expression. Thankfully, Liza greeted her, forcing Alice to look away.

She returned Liza's smile, saying, "Hi, I hope you don't mind me coming here unannounced."

"No, come in," Liza said, "I'm glad to see you. I'm sorry about yesterday. I'm just adjusting to having Tom back. I over-reacted-"

"Liza," Alice interrupted. "You don't have any reason to apologize. I understand. I meant to tell you yesterday…" Alice began, but seeing the smile on Liza's face made her stop. At the end of last night, and now this morning, Liza looked happier than she'd seemed since Alice met her. She couldn't break Liza's heart. "I'm really happy for you and your family," Alice said.

Liza's smile grew, "Thanks, and thanks for joining us

last night. It was nice having your brother along. He's an interesting man."

"Yeah, he's definitely something," Alice said, looking down at her feet. Naveed left her side and jumped onto the desk. Liza instinctively pet his back as she went to her crystal-ball reading table.

"Liza, I was hoping to use your crystal ball again this morning. I have to contact Rhys," Alice said.

"Tom wanted to talk to him, too. I couldn't reach him," Liza said, sitting down.

"Tom wanted to talk to Rhys? Why?" Alice asked.

"About that client. He's really interested in making a purchase. But Merlin's not in range or something. I can try again." Liza put her hands on the crystal ball.

Alice took a seat opposite her. Liza closed her eyes and concentrated. Alice peered into the ball, but all she could see what a mist of gray clouds. Naveed put his paw on the glass, helping. After a few seconds, he shook his furry head.

Liza opened her eyes and sighed. "Nothing. This is why Celeste always tells us we should have Untalented technology, too. Magic is many things, but it's not always reliable."

"Neither are cell phones," Alice said. She could go in on an entire conversation about awful experiences with cell service providers, but that would be giving herself away as an Untalented. Alice stood. "Thanks for trying," she said.

"No problem," Liza stood and walked her to the door. Naveed jumped down and followed Alice and Liza out. "So, are you free for lunch later?" Liza asked.

"I cant. Sorry—"

Just as Alice was about to explain, Naveed hissed in Baz's direction. Baz, mid-sip of his coffee, froze. He looked at Naveed and into the cup. Glancing between Naveed and Titania, Baz set the cup down.

Alice walked over. Liza followed, and several patrons peered in their direction. Alarm lit Titania's face.

"What is it?" Titania asked.

Baz took out his wand and tapped the ceramic three times. The liquid swirled until the brownish hue turned red. Titania's face turned the same shade as Alice, and Liza looked at her.

Alice gasped. "Poison?" she asked.

"There seems to be a lot of that in Urbana," Baz said. He glowered in Titania's direction.

"Did you drink it?" Alice asked.

"Just one sip, hardly effective," Baz said.

"How did it get into your coffee?" Liza asked.

Alice crossed her arms and accused Titania with her eyes. Titania shrunk back into her seat. With Baz, Alice, and Liza all staring at her, Titania's jaw dropped in shock.

"Why are you all looking at me like that? It wasn't me," Titania said.

"Who else?" Alice crossed her arms. Fury filled her. She wanted to shout, *"You couldn't have him, so you poisoned him?"* but she let her eyes say it for her.

Titania turned to Baz, whining, "This is insane. Surely, you don't believe I was trying to poison you?"

"Then what?" Alice asked before Baz could respond.

"It's not your business. You believe me, don't you, Baz?" Titania said.

"I..." Baz blinked as if trying to clear his thoughts.

"He's affected. Someone call for help," Alice said.

One of the patrons ran outside. Alice could see them waving to someone across the street. The bright blue of an officer's uniform came into sight in the café window.

Liza put a hand on Baz's shoulder and closed her eyes.

Her hand lit up. The distress on Baz's face began to clear, and he could speak again.

"Are you really this desperate?" Baz said, his eyes showering Titania with pity.

"It was a love potion," Liza whispered.

Alice's mouth fell open. She couldn't look at Titania with pity. All she had was anger. She knew Titania felt wounded by the world, but Alice couldn't see anything more than a spoiled rich girl who felt entitled to anything – anyone – she wanted.

Titania stood from the table. When Alice blocked her path to the door, Titania crossed her arms and held her chin up high. "I am not saying anything until I see a lawyer," Titania said.

"Which one, Titania?" Alice let the accusation seep into her tone. She knew it sounded heartless and hoped Liza didn't make the connection. But she was angry and couldn't stop herself.

"It was a love potion. That's all!" Titania said.

"It's illegal," Ron replied. He put a hand to his forehead. "How could you be so stupid? You know better than to try black magic on a ninth level mage. You were never going to get away with it."

Titania's eyes teared. She said, "Of course. Why would I think I could ever do *real* magic?" Titania sounded like a toddler who'd just lost a beauty contest.

Ron put a hand to the bridge of his nose, closed his eyes, and sighed. "By the moon, Titania, I didn't mean you can't do magic! But what you tried was risky even for an eighth level mage– not only could you be jailed for this, but you might have caused real harm."

"Where did you get the potion?" Baz asked.

"Excuse me?" Titania asked.

"You heard him," Alice said.

"Maybe I made this myself," Titania replied, holding her head up high.

Baz replied, not to Titania, but to Ron. "Love potions are tricky. They require practiced skill to extract the magic from a precisely measured set of ingredients. Regardless of skill, the recipe for black magic is not something she could have known to make on her own."

Titania held her hands to her hips, and her mouth opened as if to argue, but she couldn't find a reply. Ron stood silent for a moment, thinking. After a long while, he said, "We've had a problem with black magic lately." Ron ran a hand through his hair. Was he nervous? "Perseus' autopsy results showed poison– not a hex. Titania, we need to know where you purchased the potion." Ron stepped closer, lowering his voice. "If you don't tell us, you're practically admitting you're the one who's been mixing up black magic potions yourself."

"How dare you–"

"Titania!" The word exploded out of Ron. He grabbed his sister's hand and cuffed them together despite her protests. "This isn't a childish squabble. You're not getting a time-out; I'm taking you to jail. Get it? You can decide how long you have to stay there by either cooperating or continuing to argue."

Titania's cheeks were red and stained with tears. "I'm not saying anything until I see a lawyer," Titania repeated.

"I'm going to have to take you in," Ron said, taking out his handcuffs."

"You mean, you'd arrest me?"

"You're not really leaving me a choice," he said, reaching for her arm.

Titania pulled her hand back. "But I'm your sister! You'd arrest your own sister?"

"Sir, I can do it." Alice hadn't even seen the uniformed

officer walking into Reading & Co. just then. As he entered, Alice looked out at Magic Row, recalling what she'd seen last night.

The Essential Mage had a hidden backroom of products that Charlotte had gone in to test. If he was hiding one room, could he have been hiding another – or even a secret stash of items? Could it be that he was selling black magic potions from his shop?

It was quite a leap to make, but it made sense somehow. At least, it explained why the business was so valuable to Baz's uncle and Charlotte Fowler. The Essential Mage made a sizable profit on its own. If it was supplemented with a supply of black magic, then it might have been making double or triple what was on the books. Alice thought back to the red ledger.

Baz had wondered why his uncle had been keeping track of his tenant's sales. Maybe he had been keeping tabs on Gowdie's black market earnings. That meant Baz's uncle was a warlock, as the town had secretly suspected.

Did Baz have any friend around him who hadn't betrayed him in one way or another? Mr. Pierce hadn't if Alice's intuition served her right. And Rhys Merlin was a true friend. At least Alice hoped so. And Baz had Alice on his side, for whatever that was worth. Even if Baz had dismissed her suspicions, she had to tell someone – to protect Baz.

Alice tapped Ron on the shoulder as he handed the handcuffs to the other officer. Walking to an empty table in the front of the shop, she said, "Ron, I saw a woman at Gowdie's last night–"

Ron put a hand on Alice's shoulder, "Sorry, if this is an official complaint, will you please call the hotline? I can't deal with this right now."

"But I think Gowdie is the black market dealer you're looking for. And Charlotte Fowler might be–

"OK, Alice, I'll look into it. But I can't do anything about it right now." Ron walked outside, leaving Alice standing there feeling hopeless.

She walked back to Baz. Liza was telling him that he should go home. "You may still be affected by the potion, it's best to take the day off."

"I'm fine. And Charlotte Fowler is expecting–"

"I'll talk to her when she comes in," Liza said.

"Or better yet, Liza can contact Mr. Pierce to let him know you won't be able to make the meeting," Alice said.

"Stop, please, both of you. I'm not incapable of counteracting a spell like this. Charlotte is only in town a few days, you're both overreacting." Baz sat back down and reset his napkin on his lap. Turning toward the counter, he put his finger up to ask for another coffee.

Liza gave Alice a sympathetic look and walked back into the reading room. Naveed curled his tail around Alice's ankle and pulled as if telling her to go. Alice pulled her foot loose and walked to Baz's table.

"You know, if you were a little kinder to people who are trying to help you, you might not have a town that doesn't stick up for you when you're in trouble," Alice said.

Then she turned and walked out of the store, forgetting her breakfast for the second time that week.

SEVENTEEN

Camera Obscured

Belinda's apartment was the same as Alice remembered: A photography studio cluttered with photos. Somewhere between the lighting for cameras and the open layout kitchen was a sofa and a coffee table. Alice moved aside some pictures to make a free space on the sofa. She waited for Belinda to bring out lunch. Belinda had insisted on making an extra sandwich since Alice had come right at lunch.

"Cheese?" Belinda asked.

"Yeah, sure," Alice said. She pushed aside the photo on the coffee table as she talked. "You really don't have to go through the trouble."

"It's no trouble, I – ah, no!" Belinda said.

Alice jumped up, "What's-" the unfinished question answered itself as Alice saw Belinda's newly completed turkey sandwich hanging from Naveed's mouth.

"Down, kitty!" Belinda said. She looked back at Alice. "I'm sorry. I don't mean to yell at your cat."

"It's OK," Alice said. She frowned but wasn't angry. Naveed was a 7-foot tall man - or jinn. Alice wasn't sure how much a jinn needed to eat, but Naveed did seem to go through food at twice the rate Alice did. She should've realized he'd still be hungry.

For good or ill, Belinda's sandwich was his now.

Naveed jumped to the floor, taking *his* sandwich with him from the kitchen counters to the living room coffee table.

"Don't get the photos dirty," Alice said as they passed each other. Joining Belinda at the counter, Alice took a slice of bread out of the package. As she helped her compose the lunch, Alice continued, "Mrs. Kinjo said you found something in the photos of Baz's engagement party?"

"Well, I'm not sure how much of a 'something' I found. It seemed odd to me, and Vestra said you were looking for anything that might help Baz's case." Belinda clapped the breadcrumbs off her fingers and walked around the kitchen island. She sorted through the pictures next to Naveed on the coffee table and picked one out.

"Here it is," she said, putting the photo in front of Alice.

Alice finished the sandwich as quickly as she could, wiped her hands with a paper towel, and brought the photo close to her eyes, examining the crowd of faces.

"I don't see anything," Alice said.

Belinda slid the photo in front of Alice and pointed to a face in a crowd of partygoers on Baz's front lawn. The image was clear but the face was blurred. Alice couldn't tell who it was, nor whether it was a man or a woman.

"It's too fuzzy. I can't make it out," Alice said.

"Exactly," Belinda looked triumphant as she grabbed half of her sandwich and walked to the sofa.

Alice found a plate and took her sandwich to join Belinda. "That does happen sometimes with cameras, even if you're a good photographer," Alice said.

Belinda set the photo with the others. Then she pointed at her camera, which sat atop the table by a backdrop. "That camera is enchanted."

"I know. You showed me last time." Alice said, unconsciously clutching her charmed stone again.

Between bites of her sandwich, Belinda said, "It doesn't take blurry pictures."

Alice peered at the photo again. Naveed's cat-jinn head pressed against her cheek as he looked, too. They turned toward each other as realization spread over both of their faces.

"It's distorted because the person didn't want their image taken. They're using magic against your camera," Alice said.

Belinda nodded. "And powerful magic. I paid good money for that camera. It was a level 9 who enchanted it. It shouldn't be so easy to distort."

"That's definitely something," Alice said.

"I thought so, too, at first. Then I realized that there's another way to distort images— one that doesn't necessarily mean anything nefarious. And I don't want to go around pointing fingers for no reason."

"What's the other way?" Alice asked.

Belinda finished half of her sandwich before Alice had taken a bite of her own. Frustratingly, Belinda stood, walked into the kitchen, poured and drank a glass of water before she answered.

Both of Alice's eyebrows were raised impatiently by the time Belinda answered.

"The council members can cast joint spells on mages to disguise them for secret missions."

"Spies?"

"Sometimes. Sometimes it's just political reasons or to

protect privacy. Anyway, that may be a picture of a council member."

"Baz is on the mage council," Alice said.

"Yes, but he's in several of the pictures, and he came out just fine. So did the other local council members. They don't really have a reason to protect their identities here."

"Do you think …you're saying…" Alice tried to wrap her head around what Belinda meant.

Belinda raised her hands. "I'm not saying anything."

A safe approach, but Alice hadn't taken the safe route once since she'd entered Magic Row. She verbalized her thoughts. "Charlotte Fowler might not have come into town as late as we thought," Alice said.

Belinda sipped her water silently. Energized by the new information, Alice popped up from the sofa, grabbing the photo in one hand. She still held the plate in the other hand. Alice would have apologized for wasting the sandwich, but it had mysteriously gone missing. Naveed licked his lips beside her.

Alice walked to the kitchen and set the plate into the sink. "I'm sorry, I have to go," Alice said.

"I thought you might," Belinda answered.

"May I take this?" Alice asked, holding up the photo.

Belinda nodded. "But be careful, Alice," Belinda said, genuine concern etched on her face.

"I will," Alice said, not sure how much caution she planned to use.

Among the possibilities, she was thinking about more than just Charlotte Fowler, the council member. She was also still processing the idea of O'Crowly having a descendant in Urbana. Could it be Charlotte Fowler? Whoever it was, he or she didn't need to have the same last name as O'Crowly. Charlotte might be married for all Alice knew about her. Or she might be innocent of anything.

She wouldn't go around pointing fingers, but Alice did have to warn Baz, at least, that he was signing a deal tonight with a woman who might not be what she appeared. He seemed to be surrounded by a lot of people like that – including Alice.

"Naveed, will you-" Alice asked. She was already staring at Baz's front door before she could finish her wish.

EIGHTEEN

Baz and Betrayals

A lice used the door knocker twice, and the door flung back. It had been open before she'd gotten there. That was not a good sign. Alice looked down at Naveed, who took the first step into the foyer. Alice followed cautiously behind. Inside, Alice heard two voices: both male. One was Ron's, and he sounded distressed.

"-dodged my mages and disappeared before we could get our wands out. No one acts like that unless they're guilty," Ron was saying.

"Still, you shouldn't have searched her bag without a warrant sanctioned by the council," Baz replied.

Alice could see Ron as she entered the living room. He seethed through his teeth as he answered, "You don't need a search warrant when you have probably cause."

"It's standard procedure—

"We found a cyanide syringe in her bag! You should be happy you're off the hook. Besides, I don't need council approval for police work."

"It's a matter of courtesy," Baz said.

"Oh, it's courtesy to not honor your engagements, is it?

Without even an explanation, Baz?" Ron's dark skin reddened. He might have burst out with more anger if he and Baz hadn't both looked up and noticed Alice at that moment.

"Am I interrupting something?" Alice winced as she asked.

"No," Baz said the same time as Ron replied with a "Yes."

Baz grimaced. "Oberon and I do have some matters to discuss. Though I did plan to speak with you later. I have some idea why you've come," Baz said.

"So do I," Ron muttered, crossing his arms.

"Excuse me?" Alice asked, crossing her arms.

Baz raised an eyebrow. "Are you implying something?" he asked in a sharp tone.

Ron's eyes narrowed, and he opened his mouth as if to speak, then closed it just as quickly. He didn't need to say it. Alice could imagine what he meant.

She wasn't going to let him think that she'd come between Baz and Titania's relationship. "I've come to discuss Charlotte Fowler." Alice handed the photo to Ron.

"What am I looking at?" Ron asked.

"A distortion on a picture taken with Belinda's camera - a high-end enchanted device."

Baz reached out for the photo, which Ron handed off without argument. "An identity protection spell," Baz said.

"From the council?" Ron asked.

"If so, I'm not aware of it. And the question is what kind of identity spell is it? One for the camera lens or one for our eyes?" Baz asked.

"What do you mean?" Alice asked.

Ron interrupted, grabbing the photo for a second look. "Why hide their identity to our eyes?"

Baz ignored Ron's interruption and answered Alice's

question. "It's a spell spies use – something like a confusion spell. Weaker-willed witches and wizards might find it difficult to concentrate on the face enough to recognize the person."

"But there's a way around that. We're not like the Untalented. We can feel it if we're being influenced."

"When we know to be on guard," Baz said.

Alice caught on. "It was a party. None of us was prepared for an intruder."

Ron held the photo up, as if he could shed light on the situation if he held it at the right angle. "You think this is Charlotte Fowler?" Ron asked.

"I…," She hesitated, her resolve waning. Naveed rubbed against her leg, encouraging her to continue. "I think she may have come earlier than she let on. When I was in The Essential Mage earlier, I overheard Charlotte talking to Oliver Gowdie. She hinted that she knew Gowdie had made up the stories about Baz, and she knew the real story about who was arguing with whom the night before. I assumed she'd heard it from the butler or the maid, but-"

"But she might have heard it for herself at the party," Ron said.

"Something seems wrong about that. Even if Charlotte had arrived in Urbana early, why risk being seen at the party? Merlin would have seen through her enchantment, even I might have-"

"We all know you're extra-talented." Ron cut Baz off. He held the picture up, saying. "I'll look into this."

Ron walked toward the door without another word, disappearing before he'd made it to the foyer. Baz jaw set tight while Ron made his exit. He kept staring at the empty air until Alice's concern caught his eye.

Alice gave Baz a half-hearted smile. "Everything OK?"

Baz ran a hand through his black hair and sighed. "I'm sure you know I broke the engagement with Miss Knight."

"I assumed as much. That must have been difficult. I'm sorry," Alice said, her heart fluttering so much she worried Baz could see that she was not sorry at all.

Titania had been wrong for him. Baz was free now to find the right person. So, why did he look so miserable?

Baz faced the fireplace. His eyes were not their usual icy blue. The fire twisted, squeezed, and suffocated his natural color until all Alice could see was flame.

"Difficult, yes, but was it right?" Baz said.

"You think you shouldn't have broken it off with Titania?" Alice wondered if it was him speaking or if the love potion had some effect after all.

Baz looked at Alice, searching her eyes with more emotion than she'd seen in him before. "Talent is inherited – but it only grows if one believes in oneself. The wick is there, but igniting it…" Baz shook his head.

He was talking about Titania, that was clear. But Alice was applying it to herself. Magic was inherited, but she'd never believed – not truly – that she had magic. What if her belief was all that was missing?

"I don't know if I could be that for someone," Baz interrupted her thoughts.

"Be what?" Alice asked.

"The spark," Baz said, walking closer to Alice. She braced herself— for what she wasn't sure, but Baz stopped his advance just close enough to catch the spice scent of his cologne.

"To spark the magic in someone else takes patience, belief, even…love," Baz said, his eyes capturing hers.

Alice swallowed, her throat going dry. Her palms felt

sweaty, her heart beat like she'd just finished a marathon. Was Baz going to...*kiss* her?

Baz's blue eyes searching Alice's face. "Have I made a mistake?" Baz asked.

"No," Alice said. Then she blinked, puzzled by the question. "What mistake are we talking about?" Alice asked.

Baz pulled away. "Titania is a Knight. Whatever her power level, her family is more than talented enough to ward off a powerful warlock."

"You're talking about protecting Urbana," Alice realized.

"Hex told me what you've no doubt come to say – that a warlock, perhaps an O'Crowly, is in Urbana."

"I think it might be worse than that," Alice said.

"Which makes it all the more imperative that an alliance is created." Baz looked away.

"A marriage alliance? Isn't that a little medieval?" Alice asked.

Baz walked toward the fireplace. He put a hand on the mantle, facing away from Alice as he said, "It's not just the alliance. A Knight and Delvaux child would have powerful magic. If not O'Crowly now, there will be another warlock later. Another creator mage might destroy the world."

"That's going a little far, isn't it?" Alice said, trying to lighten the mood.

Baz turned around and stared if anything more upset than before. "How can *you* say that?"

Alice froze. Why the emphasis on "you?" Was her cover blown?

"After what your family sacrificed, I would think you know more than anyone what a creator Warlock– what an O'Crowly– can do," Baz said.

"My family," Alice said. Despite herself and for reasons

she couldn't fully explain, her eyes began to tear. Alice hated crying. Crying made one weak. Tears had made her a target in the orphanage when she'd had no parents to comfort her.

Baz reached out, hesitated, then wiped a tear from her cheek. The tenderness made the tears flow harder.

Baz waited for her to regain her composure then said, "I'm sorry for what you lost. But the power of your once-great house still flows in you. If you were a Creator mage—"

"I'm not," Alice said. She exhaled, relieved to at least admit she wasn't a level ten.

"I know," Baz said, stepping back. They stood a few seconds, staring at one another, something unspoken between them. Alice was sure Baz was going to confess he felt it, too. She wasn't sure she was ready to hear it. "You had some information to give me?" Baz asked.

Alice cleared her throat. "Yes. I didn't want to alarm Ron, especially if I'm wrong. But there's another possibility of who is in that picture."

Baz's eyes widened. "O'Crowly," he said as if reading her mind.

Alice nodded. "Tell me I'm jumping to conclusions; I'd really like to sleep soundly tonight."

Across the room, Hex transformed. Naveed left his position beside Alice. Hex shot him a glance. She walked toward Alice, saying, "I think your conclusion is more than likely."

"If that's the case, he has infiltrated Magic Row's community," Alice said.

"*That* is a leap," Baz said. "Even I do not know every person in town, but we are a small enough community that I would notice a creator mage among us. He might have come to Urbana for the first time last night."

Baz and Alice looked at each other, sharing the same thought.

"What if O'Crowly's descendant…" Alice began.

"Is Charlotte Fowler," Baz concluded.

"It is possible," Hex said.

"We have to find her," Alice began walking toward the door.

Baz caught Alice's shoulder. He let go as soon as he touched her. "The police are already searching for her," Baz said.

"But they don't know what they're dealing with," Alice said.

"I will warn Ron," Baz said.

"And Naveed and I will search Urbana for a trail of O'Crowly's magic," Hex said.

"What do I do, other than toss and turn all night waiting for you guys?" Alice said.

"We will find her," Baz managed a smile, adding, "You can sleep well tonight."

NINETEEN

Runaway Puck

S leeping was impossible with a warlock on the loose in Urbana. Alone in her apartment, Alice sat on the couch where Naveed should have been sleeping and clicked on the TV. She hated to admit that she'd gotten used to having a jinn in her living room. She did get better rest hearing her all-powerful protector snoring steps away from her door.

Alice was sure a jinn wouldn't have a deviated septum. He was doing it on purpose just to annoy her, but Naveed swore otherwise. She missed the sound now. Alice pulled her knees up and hugged her legs as she watched the "one time offer" infomercial for…something. She wasn't really listening.

She was hoping Naveed was safe. Wishing he would catch Charlotte and praying she and Baz were right about her being the warlock, O'Crowly.

At about two in the morning, Alice fell asleep, curled up hugging a pillow. She jumped when a knocking on her front door startled her awake. Disoriented, Alice mistook the loud cry of *"Samantha!"* on the TV set for reality. She looked around for the yelling man, only to realize the culprit was the lead actor in a black and white episode of *"Bewitched."* Alice switched off the TV show and smoothed out her hair.

Shielding her eyes from the morning sun, Alice looked at the clock: 6 am. The pounding grew loud enough to match Naveed's temper. It couldn't be Naveed, though. He would have just appeared indoors. For a moment, Alice wondered if she should answer since it could be anyone on the other side. She doubted a warlock would be so polite as to knock.

"I'm coming," Alice said. She wrapped her robe tightly around her waist and opened the door an inch, keeping the chain secured. "Puck, what are you doing here?" she asked.

Puck ran a hand through his hair, distraught. "I didn't know who else to go to," Puck said.

"What's wrong?" Alice unlatched the chain and let Puck through.

"They're arresting Mr. Gowdie," Puck said, pacing in the living room.

"For what?" Alice asked as she sat on a bench at the kitchen island.

"They're saying he sells black-market magic," Puck said.

Alice scratched her head and tucked a strand of hair behind her ear, trying not to say what she was thinking.

"He doesn't," Puck said, scoffing.

"How well do you know Mr. Gowdie?" Alice asked.

"Really well...I mean, well enough. He was one of the only people in this town that ever gave me a chance. I worked for him a little."

"You worked at The Essential Mage?" Alice asked.

Puck lowered himself to the edge of the sofa. "No, not

exactly. I ran errands for him, delivering orders to customers who couldn't pick them up. And getting things he needed."

"Like stealing?" Alice asked.

"No! I picked stuff up for him," Puck said.

"What kind of "stuff?"" Alice asked.

"I don't know. Packages. I never looked, but they weren't illegal." Puck was adamant.

Alice rose. "All right. Give me a minute to get ready, and we'll go."

"Where's your familiar?" Puck asked.

He meant the cat-jinn, whom he knew was magical. He hadn't quite guessed Naveed was a jinn. He looked around the sofa.

"He's out. You know how cats are." Alice kept her tone light, but she was worried about him being gone for so long. What if O'Crowly, Charlotte, or whoever the warlock was, had gotten to him?

Changing quickly and not even bothering to put on make-up, Alice came out of the room within minutes. Puck held out his hand, which Alice took, and they were instantly transported to Many Treasures. From there, Puck and Alice walked across the street to A Witch's Thrift Shop, where they could watch the flashing lights of the police cars and the crowd forming from a fair distance away.

Seconds in, Ron came out the front door to the Essential Mage, leading a handcuffed Oliver Gowdie to his police car. Puck made fists with his hands and made as if to run to Gowdie's aid. Alice grabbed his arm.

"There's nothing we can do," she said.

Puck opened his mouth to argue, but instead of saying a word, he let out a frustrated breath and yanked his arm away. He ran back toward Many Treasures, disappearing as he went.

"Puck!" Alice called out.

"Save your breath," Celeste said. She walked around A Witch's Thrift Shop and threw a bag of trash in the bin. Then she walked over to Alice. "I'm sorry to say that it's probably best that he makes a run for it."

"What? Why?" Alice asked.

Celeste sighed. "Everyone knows Puck ran errands for Gowdie. It was probably the closest thing to honest work Puck did, only now it turns out it wasn't so honest if it was black magic all along."

"Puck may not have known that," Alice said.

"Whether he knew it or not, he'd be on Ron's shortlist of people to question," Celeste said.

Alice winced. "Even I accused him of stealing this morning. He needs people on his side who don't just assume he's guilty of something."

"Maybe I could before he stole from me," Celeste said.

"Puck did his community service for that," Alice said.

"Yes, one weekend's worth because Gowdie had his lawyers claim Puck was coerced into the theft. Every time we can actually prove it was Puck, Gowdie comes in with lawyers or pays a fine for him. He's like Puck's guardian angel. Now that he's gone, it wouldn't surprise me if Puck runs away."

"You think he really would?" Alice asked, mortified that she might have contributed to Puck feeling like he had nowhere else to turn.

She wondered about it for the rest of the morning. Alice called around town at places where Puck might be, not that she was prying into Puck's life. She just would have felt better if she knew that Celeste was wrong…and if Alice could apologize for her accusation.

When Naveed returned at 1pm with no news on Charlotte's whereabouts, panic took hold of Alice. Baz and Hex had gone to an emergency meeting to inform the council that Charlotte may be a warlock on the run. If that was true, Alice wanted Puck safely out of the streets. She sent Naveed out on the prowl for the runaway.

Puck still wasn't back by dinner time. That was when Alice voiced her concern. Mrs. Kinjo checked the guest room to find Puck's belongings gone, confirming Alice's worst fears.

"Couldn't he just be at a friend's house?" Vestra asked.

"His friends are all troublemakers. I told him to stay away from them," Alice said.

"Boys never listen," Mrs. Kinjo sat on the upstairs sofa, pulling Naveed into his arms. He squirmed a little, but he let her stroke his head without a growl. She needed comfort, and he was it right now. He took it like a cat, curling into her lap and placing a paw on her resting arm.

Eric grabbed his jacket. "I'm going to look for him."

"I'll come, too," Alice and Vestra said in unison. Alice looked at Vestra, rethinking.

"You guys have that stargazing party, don't you?" Alice said.

"It's another meteor shower, but it's no big deal. There will always be another," Eric said, pulling his jacket on. "I just got used to having a little brother around. Don't want to lose him now."

"Shouldn't we call the police? I mean, this is like a missing person thing, isn't it?" Vestra asked.

"You have to wait 24 hours. I saw that on TV," Mrs. Kinjo said.

"You guys take the west side of main street, I'll take the east," Alice said.

"Alone?" Vestra asked.

"I'll take fluffy with me," Alice said. Naveed jumped off of Mrs. Kinjo's lap.

He and Alice walked downstairs. As Eric and Vestra left, Naveed transformed.

"Should we leave Mrs. Kinjo here?" Naveed said.

"We can't take her with us," Alice said.

"I mean, should she be here alone? We already know someone broke in and stole the wand."

Alice grinned. "You care about her," she said.

Naveed transformed back into a cat and growled. In the storefront window, lights flashed as a car stopped right outside the door. Alice's first thought was that Naveed was right to be worried. She wasn't sure what she would do if a warlock burst through the door.

On the other hand, she was almost certain warlocks didn't drive police cars. Relief was the first emotion Alice felt on seeing Ron, followed by gut-twisting guilt. Even though Ron's wildly-flung accusations were wrong, he wasn't off the mark about her attraction to Baz. Everyone on Magic Row must have seen that by now.

Alice braced herself as Ron walked through the door. Naveed jumped up on the counter to help her if Ron wanted to hex her or— more likely— to get a good show from the upcoming argument. The door dinged, and Ron greeted Alice silently with a forced smile.

"I'm here about Puck," Ron said.

"He doesn't know anything about Gowdie's illegal–"

"I'm here because I heard you're calling around looking for him," Ron interrupted. "Is he missing?" Ron asked.

"Yeah. I'm going out to look for him," Alice said.

"I'll go with you," Ron said.

"I don't need any help. Thanks for coming," Alice said, letting it show that she was hurt.

Ron sighed. "Look, I…I was out of line earlier. I don't blame you for anything. I just want to help, OK?"

Ron seemed genuine. Naveed meowed softly as if giving Ron his approval.

"OK," Alice said. She petted Naveed's head, adding, "You stay here, Fluffy." Naveed batted her hand away with his paw like he always did.

Alice and Ron made their way into the dreary night. The knot in Alice's stomach relaxed, though not all the way. She still worried Puck was out there with a warlock on the loose, but she'd feel better knowing Naveed would protect Mrs. Kinjo should anything happen to her. If Baz was right, the Knights had powerful magic of their own, so Alice would be safe with Ron. Eric had Vestra with her, and Alice doubted any warlock would recognize them, so Eric would be all right, too. All Alice needed to do was find Puck.

"Did he leave of his own accord?" Ron asked as they sat in the car.

"He's still a minor," Alice said, fastening her seatbelt.

"He's emancipated. There's nothing I can do, and he's not wanted for any crime at the moment." Ron shrugged his shoulders. Seeing the concern on Alice's face, he unlocked the car doors. "All right, hop in. It wouldn't hurt to check around the neighborhood."

"Thanks," Alice said.

They drove around the block. Alice kept her eyes out the window until the silence between them grew uncomfortable. It wouldn't do any good to talk about what was really making Ron angry or distant. Whether it was Liza or Titania and Baz, Ron wouldn't want to hear Alice's perspective. Alice focused on Puck.

"You said Puck was emancipated– I thought he was an orphan?" Alice asked.

"He had an aunt and uncle; he's been emancipated from them since he was sixteen. Legally, that means he's allowed to go anywhere on his own," Ron said.

"What do you know about the Morgans?" Alice asked.

Ron sighed. "Look, it's nice that you're helping Puck out. Many of us tried when he first showed up last year, but this is what Puck does. Don't let it get to you if he decided to leave town."

"Don't you feel bad for him, Ron? I mean, his family situation had to be tough for him to be granted emancipation, don't you think?" Alice said.

"Yeah, it was awful," Ron said.

"Awful, how?" Alice asked. Ron didn't answer, so Alice pressed the subject. "Ron, I don't think any of us can really help him if we don't really know his history. I only want to help."

Ron kept driving in silence for a minute. Turning another corner, Ron finally sighed and gave in. "Puck's name isn't 'Morgan,'" Ron said.

"What is it?" Alice asked.

Ron sighed. "If I told you, well, *you* might have a heart of gold, but if everyone else in Magic Row knew, they might run him out of town just for that."

"They already seem to dislike him," Alice said.

"There's a wide gap between dislike and hate," Ron said.

"And a narrow bridge linking them, if a last name is enough to cross the distance," Alice said.

"If you heard what it is, you might agree," Ron said.

"It can't be as bad as that." Alice refused to believe it.

"Oh yeah? Even if it's O'Crowly?" Ron asked.

"Yes, even then," Alice said.

Ron locked his eyes on her and raised his eyebrows as

if waiting for her to get his point. Alice's draw dropped. "No," she whispered. "It really is O'Crowly?"

Ron nodded.

"How did you find out?" Alice asked.

"I'm a police officer. That's what I do, especially with troublemakers in town," Ron said.

"But, he created an alternate identity? Where did he come up with the name Morgan?" Alice asked.

"Morgan is his mother's maiden name. O'Crowly is his father's. He's from the same family as the level 10 wizard – he might even be the original O'Crowly's grandson, but I don't have info from that far back," Ron said.

"So, he decided to change his name when he came to Magic Row. He probably just didn't want the stigma," Alice realized.

"He came into town with more than just a stigma if what Baz says is true."

"He told you about O'Crowly?" Alice asked.

"Yep," Ron said. "Would have been nice to hear it direct from the source?"

"Sorry. I didn't want to panic anyone. What are you going to do?" Alice asked.

"That's only up to a level 10 mage to decide."

"Rhys Merlin decides?" Alice asked. "What has he said?"

"He said he'd do whatever was necessary."

"What does that mean?"

"It means Magic Row is about to become a battleground in an all-out war among Creator mages," Ron said.

"That can't be good for business," Alice joked. Laughter was better than crying wasn't it?

"No, it's not good. Nothing about a power-hungry tyrant is ever a 'good' thing," Ron said. He wasn't laughing.

TWENTY

A Hex Upon Her

Forty-minutes into their drive, Ron and Alice passed a convenience store with a patrol car flashing its lights in the parking lot. Ron parked on the street. He grabbed his handheld radio and got out.

"Looks like an attempted robbery. Stay here," Ron said through the window.

He opened the car door and walked over to the other officers.

Alice sat for a moment, watching the officers. She looked away, her mind wandering back to Puck. Cars and people passed, not one of them resembling the red-headed teen. Then Alice had a horrible thought. Puck wouldn't have committed robbery, would he?

Alice got out of the car and began walking toward the convenience store. She surveyed the scene, looking for any hint of Puck. Out of the corner of her eye, she caught sight of a familiar face. Charlotte Fowler stumbled like a drunk woman, her gray business suit was ripped, and her hair fell out of it bun. She didn't look like a threat, but like a woman who had just lost a fight.

Alice walked around the police cars. She hastened turned around the corner of the store to where Charlotte leaned against the wall. Charlotte had her hand on her forehead, seemingly dazed.

"Ms. Fowler?" Alice asked.

Charlotte looked up, her eyes widening on seeing Alice look at her. She pushed herself off the wall and turned around, ready to bolt. Alice instinctively grabbed her shoulder. Charlotte screeched.

"Shh, it's OK. I'm not going to hurt you," Alice said. She hoped Charlotte didn't suspect she was Untalented and call her bluff. Just in case, she added, "There are about five officers around the corner, though sand at least one of them is a Knight, so you might want to turn yourself in."

Charlotte turned back around, looking dazed. "A knight?" Charlotte asked. She looked behind Alice, her eyes, though searching, seemed vacant.

"Are you all right, Ms. Fowler?" Alice asked.

"Why are you calling me that? Is that my name?" Charlotte asked.

Alice looked at Naveed. He stared back at her with the same shocked expression. "You don't remember who you are?" Alice asked.

"I'm," Charlotte hesitated. She adjusted her bun, trying unsuccessfully to tuck her hair back into place. "Don't be silly. I'm Ms. Fowler...Ms. um...something Fowler...." She looked at Alice for guidance.

"Charlotte," Alice said, filling in the blanks.

"Of course, yes: Charlotte Fowler." Charlotte regained her regal posture, looking confidently as if her lapse in memory was a momentary glitch. But then she asked, "My dear, would you be so kind as to tell me what I'm doing here?"

"Freeze." A voice came from behind Alice. Ron had his

wand pointed at Charlotte and one hand on his radio. "We've got her," he said.

Charlotte turned and ran. Alice blocked her way.

"He's trying to help you," Alice said as evenly as she could. She shouted over her shoulder, "It's OK, Ron. She's all right. You're all right." Alice repeated more softly to Charlotte. Ron came around Alice, forcing her out of the way.

"Put your hands—"

"Ron!" Alice interrupted his command.

"Move aside," Ron said. He grabbed Charlotte's arm, fastening handcuffs onto her wrists roughly.

"What did I do?" Charlotte sounded like she was holding back tears as she demanded, "Let me go!"

"I don't think she's your suspect. Can't you see she's confused?" Alice said.

"Now's not the time." Ron tried to move around Alice.

"Her memory has been hexed." Alice stood in his way.

Two wizard officers appeared, moving in on Charlotte. Charlotte stomped on Ron's foot and attempted to run. Ron was unphased. He grabbed Charlotte's arm and held her until the officers could take hold of her.

"Read her her rights and take her in," Ron said.

"Ron," Alice started.

Ron slid his wand into a slot on his belt Alice hadn't noticed was there before. "I hear you, Alice, but if she's hexed, she'll still have to be taken in and treated, even if she's innocent."

"But this proves she's innocent, right? I mean, who would hex her except the real killer?" Alice asked.

Ron shrugged. "She could have done this to herself. Maybe she only hexed a small part of her memory. Maybe she's acting. Or maybe Gowdie was her accomplice, and he hexed her."

"You arrested Gowdie this morning," Alice said.

"She's been missing since yesterday," Ron said.

"Yeah, I guess he could have hexed her then," Alice said.

"I thought you were as suspicious of him as anyone, or even more so," Ron said as they walked back to the car.

"That was before I saw a woman at Gowdie's shop last night," Alice said.

"I hate to say that it could have been my sister, buying her love potion," Ron remarked.

"That's what I thought, too, now I'm not sure," Alice said.

"We'll sort it out at the station." Ron reassured her as he opened his car door. He stopped before sitting inside. "Did Eric and Vestra have any luck finding him?"

Alice took her phone out of her pocket and looked. "No messages," she said.

"OK, I think we need to call it a night. I'll give you a ride home, and we can look for Puck again in the morning," Ron sat in the car.

Alice looked around one last time. She knew this area. The World Cultures museum was just the next street over, so Alice opened the door. "I'm going to keep looking," she said as she took her purse out and closed the door.

Ron rolled down the window. "I won't stop you, but Alice, I think you have to face the fact that Puck was never going to stay here forever. You tried, but you can't save everyone." Ron started the engine drove down the street.

The closer Alice walked toward the museum, the more confident she was that she would find Puck. Walking around the entrance to the side of the building, Alice found a flickering street lamp casting eerie light onto the image of a boy in a hoodie. She smiled, glad to see her suspicions confirmed.

"Puck?" Alice asked as she neared the boy.

The kid looked up. Pulling the hoodie off his head, Puck revealed himself. Alice crossed her arms.

"Do you realized how many people are out looking for you? Mrs. Kinjo is worried sick, Eric is missing his stargazing party," Alice chastised.

"How'd you find me?" Puck asked. He looked drained and tired, and unless it was Alice's imagination, his eyes were puffy and red like he'd been fighting tears.

Alice sighed and sat next to him on the curb. "I figured a runaway needs a source of income. I remembered Mr. Coulson's offer. So, did you do a gig?"

"'It's not in the budget.' That's what he said." Puck threw a rock across the parking lot like he was skipping stone on a lake.

"I'm sorry." Alice put a hand on his shoulder.

"Yeah, Coulson apologized, too," Puck said.

Alice hated to admit she knew that would happen. Mr. Coulson was a people-pleaser, which meant he didn't always mean what he said. While he did want to hire Alice, his offer to Puck was probably a matter of in-the-moment politeness.

"I knew it was too good to be true," Puck said.

"I can talk to Mr. Coulson if you want," Alice said.

"No, I don't need him," Puck said. He threw another rock.

"Like you don't need us anymore?" Alice asked.

Puck shrugged. "Why should I stay? You keep thinking I'm a thief. You won't give me a chance."

"Each time you break someone's trust it's harder to repair it," Alice said.

"I haven't stolen anything since Mrs. Kinjo went off on me," Puck said.

"That was yesterday," Alice said. Puck threw another

rock– with more force this time. "I can't promise I'll never suspect you of anything ever again, trust takes time. But I know trust works both ways, so I promise you this: I will always hear you out and give you as many chances as you need to set your life straight – so will Mrs. Kinjo and Eric. And whatever happens with Mr. Gowdie, we'll have your back. You just have to be honest and willing to change," Alice said.

Puck nodded.

"So, are you still running away?" Alice asked.

"No, let's just go." Puck stood up.

"You mean you're staying?" Alice stood, too.

"I guess," Puck said.

Alice offered him her hand, and he took it. "Why don't you do the honors and take us back too Many Treasures?" Alice asked.

Puck pulled out his wand and waved. The scene around them fell away, and in its place, the walls of the antique store constructed themselves. Alice and Puck were now standing in front of the counter at Many Treasures.

Vestra gasped. Eric, who was standing by the cash register with the phone pressed to his hear, set down the receiver and walked around the counter. He pulled Puck into a hug.

"What's the big idea, leaving us like that?" Eric asked.

Puck stood speechless, almost seeming to tear up by the surprise of the hug.

"He was a little upset, but I think he's over it now," Alice said.

"Glad you didn't run away," Vestra said.

Puck seemed to snap out of it. He leaned on the cash register. "Yeah, well, maybe next time. I guess you're stuck with me for now," Puck said.

"We better go tell, Mrs. Kinjo." Vestra reached out for Eric.

Eric took her hand and walked with her. He paused at the stairway. "Are you coming?" he asked.

"I have a question for him, I'll send him up in a minute if that's OK," Alice said. She waited for Eric and Vestra to leave before she asked. "Is there a reason why you can't stay in one place longer than three months?"

"Who told you that?" Puck asked.

"Is it true?" Alice asked.

"Maybe," Puck said.

"You stayed here longer. Why?"

"I don't know," Puck said. After a few seconds of Alice staring at him, he explained, "The people are nicer here. I mean, you came looking for me–" Puck looked Alice in the eye– "No one's ever done that before. No one whom I wanted to find me," Puck said.

"What do you mean?" Alice asked.

Puck shook his head. "Never mind. I should get upstairs," Puck said.

He passed Naveed on the staircase. Naveed gave him a "meow" and jumped into Puck's arms. Puck fell into the wall. His bag tumbled from his shoulders. Puck laughed.

"It's good to see you, too," he said, and he set Naveed back onto the floor.

Naveed helped Puck scoop up a few items that had fallen to the ground. He grabbed a notebook with his mouth. When Puck opened the bag, Naveed plunged the notebook, and his whole face, inside. Puck pulled Naveed out and shoved the rest of his items back into it. Then he closed up the bag and said, "Thanks, see you later," before running upstairs.

Naveed walked to Alice, caught her ankle with his tail, and shifted them to Alice's apartment. Once inside,

Naveed transformed into his jinn form. He sat on the couch, a taco appearing in one hand as he flicked on the TV with the other.

"You weren't just giving Puck a hug, were you? What did you find?" Alice asked.

"There was no wand in his bag. He's clear," Naveed said.

"How did you know Puck was an O'Crowly?" Alice asked.

Naveed raised an eyebrow. "I didn't. I just know he's a thief," Naveed said.

"Well, he won't be one anymore. I think we have a good O'Crowly on our side," Alice said.

"That'll be something," Naveed replied.

"Yeah, you know. I think it will be. Good night," Alice said. She knew she should be worried about having an O'Crowly at the Kinjos, but Alice had looked in Puck's eyes, and she hadn't seen a warlock. Puck was just a kid who needed a family, and Alice was glad that he was home safe. Knowing that Alice could sleep soundly tonight.

TWENTY-ONE

Thrift Shop Talk

R on's theory– according to Eric, who heard it from Vestra, who heard it from a friend, who heard it from her boyfriend, who was one of the officer mages who helped Ron make the arrest– was that Charlotte Fowler was guilty. Further, she had an accomplice. Either Charlotte and her accomplice hatched their plan from the beginning, or they had teamed up after Charlotte Fowler came to town. If Ron's mystery culprit was Gowdie, then the people responsible for killing Perseus, stealing O'Crowly's wand, and running a black magic market operation in Urbana were behind bars. It seemed to fit. Except that Alice couldn't see how Charlotte was faking the fear and helplessness Alice saw in her eyes the night before.

Clarity was something Celeste could offer. Talking to her always made Alice understand the magic community better. Alice took an early break in her morning shift, left Naveed with Eric at Many Treasures, and made her way to A Witch's Thrift Shop to talk things over with Celeste. There was only one customer this morning, and he was already walking to the counter to check out.

"Ron?" Alice asked.

"Alice, did you find Puck, or do we still need to go looking today?" Ron said.

"I found him, but if you're going to question him—"

"Not today. I've got to get the paperwork done on Ms. Fowler's arrest and more digging to do on the investigation," Ron said.

"I thought it was all wrapped up and you were convinced Charlotte and Gowdie are guilty," Alice said.

"Yes, they are guilty— of separate things," Ron said.

"They worked together and turned on each other, right?" Alice said.

He leaned away from the counter, "Between you and me, you saw how Ms. Fowler was acting last night – I think she was faking that memory hex. We'll do an m-trace today, just to make sure."

"Why would she fake a memory hex?"

"To put us off her trail. She wants to take the blame off of her. Charlotte Fowler brought a briefcase of magical potions to Urbana. What possible reason could she have brought that except to poison Perseus?" Ron asked.

"I saw her bring that briefcase to Gowdie's—"

Ron interrupted Alice. "So, you think she and Gowdie were in on it? Now she's trying to shift blame onto Gowdie alone. It makes perfect sense." Ron said.

"Unless he really hexed her," Alice said.

Ron stopped at the counter and put his basket of items down for Celeste to start scanning. He turned to Alice, "I'll look into it," Ron said.

Alice shook her head. "Why didn't you already think about it?"

"Alice," Celeste interrupted in a warning tone.

Alice studied Ron's face. He had a tiny bead of sweat

dripping down his temple and he was avoiding Alice's eyes. "You have a suspect in mind, don't you?" Alice said.

Ron didn't answer. He did, however, shift uncomfortably on his toes and ask Celeste, "How much is it?" before she was done ringing him up.

"It's not me is it?" Alice asked.

Ron chuckled. "No, you're not a suspect," Ron said.

Alice didn't know what else to say. Celeste gave Alice the side-eye, silently telling her to stay out of the investigation. Alice looked away, wondering how she could coax the truth out of Ron. That was when Alice noticed the pile of Ron's purchases. They didn't seem like the type of items Ron would buy.

"What's with all the crystals?" Alice asked, hoping small talk would help her dig the truth out of him.

"Titania is 'horribly traumatized'– her words– by her time in jail. She needs to realign her energy before she comes home," Ron said.

"And such a shame Gowdie's is closed, so you have to buy them here," Vestra said, coming from around the aisle and walking over to them.

"Better get ready for another busy day." Celeste gave Vestra a meaningful stare, trying to redirect her from joining the conversation.

"Hazel and I are on it," Vestra gave a mock-salute.

"Did someone say my name?" Hazel walked up to the counter, too.

Ron cleared his throat. "Hi, Hazel, how's your mom, your family, I mean?"

"Good! Mom told dad she wants a little time to readjust as a family before we move."

"You were thinking to, uh, leave?" Ron asked.

"Not if I can help it," Hazel beamed.

"I hope you stay. We love having you here at the shop,

but I'm sure you'll be fine wherever you go," Celeste said, more comfortable now that the conversation had turned away from the investigation. She bagged Ron's crystals and said, "That'll be $12.47."

Ron looked down to take out his change but kept glancing at Hazel and Alice like he wanted to speak. When Hazel started to walk away, he asked quickly, "So, you all had dinner the other night?" His nonchalant tone fooled Hazel, but not Alice.

Vestra gave a salty smile, wiggling her eyebrows when Ron couldn't see her. Alice tried not to laugh. Hazel remained oblivious.

Bursting into a smile, Hazel said, "It was family night. We used to do them once a week before…" Hazel's smile faded. She gave a faraway look, watching old memories play out in her head. Alice knew what that was like, remembering a time before a tragedy.

"Hazel, could you check the shipment of fliers for typos? You're good at spelling, right?" Vestra guided Hazel away from the conversation.

Celeste gave Ron a sympathetic look as she gave him his change. "I'm afraid they are back together for good. You'll have to let this one go," Celeste said.

"Let what go? No, I…I was just asking." Ron cleared his throat. "It's good to see a family, you know, reunited," Ron said.

Alice felt a knot tightening in her stomach. She once thought Ron was just a playboy. He seemed like the much better match now, the way he cared about the kids, how he looked at Liza, and stepping out of the way for Tom, he surprised Alice by being a gentleman. She hoped she was misjudging Tom the way she had misunderstood Ron in the beginning. Tom was, at least, helping Baz with the accusation of murder.

In her back pocket, Alice's phone dinged. She took it out of her pocket and had to roll her eyes when she saw who had sent her a text. She hadn't even known Tom had her number. Liza must have passed it along to him.

"Still not willing to part with the wand?" The text from Tom read. Alice shook her head and dropped the phone back into her pocket. She wasn't going to bother to answer.

Ron grabbed his bag of crystals for Titania and turned around. As if rethinking, he looked back at Alice. "You know, I shouldn't be saying this, but I do need more proof before I can dismiss from Baz as a suspect."

"Don't you mean you need proof to make Baz a suspect?" Alice asked.

Ron remained silent.

"You have proof, don't you?" Alice said, in almost a whisper.

Ron moved away from the register, much good it did. Celeste had ears like a bat. And Vestra's feet carried her toward gossip like wings.

"There was a syringe in Charlotte's bag with the Rose Hospital logo on it," Ron said.

"Yeah, I overhead you the other day. It had traces of cyanide in it. That's bad for Charlotte— not Baz. And I don't think it's hers either, I think Gowdie planted it there," Alice said.

"It had Baz's fingerprints on it," Ron said, stunning Alice into silence. He added, "It's not magic, but it's still counts as strong evidence."

Alice stood speechless staring until Ron's face went out of focus. An eternity passed before she could bring herself to speak. Even then it was disjointed.

"I—how—that's not..." Alice took a breath. "That can't be true," Alice whispered.

"I'm not saying he's guilty, but we have to follow the

proof: We have the fingerprints and the fact that a memory hex needs to be performed by at least a ninth level mage. I don't want to believe it, but Baz is our most likely suspect."

"Baz is innocent," Alice said, simply because she didn't know what else to say.

"Bring me proof." Ron's voice was firm, but the way he raised his eyebrows softened the statement. It wasn't an argument, it was a request. He was asking for Alice's help.

Not officially, of course. Ron couldn't ask a citizen to investigate a police matter. But everyone in town thought Alice was a level nine mage. Now was the time to act like one.

Only Alice didn't know where to start. As soon as her shift was over, she went to a literal drawing board back at her apartment. Taking her vision board off the wall, Alice cleaned off the whiteboard behind it. She searched through the kitchen drawers for a marker.

"I don't get why you're doing this. It's Gowdie, plain and simple. Perseus was poisoned, so Gowdie's alibi doesn't matter and Charlotte was likely his partner and he turned on her," Naveed said, sitting backward on the couch to face the board.

"Ron needs proof. And I don't think Charlotte is guilty." Alice said as she uncapped a blue marker.

"Humans are always guilty of something," Naveed shrugged.

"We're not as bad as you think. Although in Gowdie's case you might be right. But Charlotte is another story. I don't think she came to town early, and I don't think it was her we saw at Gowdie's that night. I think that was Titania," Alice said.

"You didn't like her, and suddenly you think she's innocent?" Naveed asked.

"You know how Gowdie used a potion to test for black

magic in the soil? What if Charlotte brought the vials of potions to Urbana to do the same thing? She could have been checking Gowdie's inventory the same way," Alice said.

"So, she's not in on it with Gowdie," Naveed said.

"Gowdie is the guilty party," Alice said, feeling pretty good about her conclusion. She added, "Hex's m-trace found that whoever stole the wand had O'Crowly's magic, which means O'Crowly is out there somewhere pretending to be someone else. Do you think Gowdie is O'Crowly?" Alice asked.

"Puck is an O'Crowly. The simplest explanation is that he he stole the wand for Gowdie," Naveed said.

"I can't keep accusing him," Alice said.

"He might not have known why he was doing it," Naveed suggested. Naveed laid back on the sofa as if he were talking to a therapist and said, "Humans are so easy to see through. Gowdie had it out for Perseus. Maybe he knew Perseus was trying to turn him in for his black magic market. Gowdie also doesn't particularly like Baz, so he wouldn't be heartbroken to let Baz take the fall."

Alice went along with it, adding, "Gowdie gets Baz to touch the syringe while Baz and Titania are shopping for their ring and filling in their wedding wishlist. Then, when Charlotte went in to expose Gowdie's black market, he hexed her and slipped the syringe in her bag."

"Then Gowdie finds out about O'Crowly's possessions and hires Puck to steal them," Naveed said.

"But how did he know about O'Crowly's wand?" Alice said.

"You heard Tom. Everyone on Magic Row knows," Naveed said.

"But who's the one who has been spreading the most gossip lately," Alice said.

"Gowdie can't be O'Crowly. He's been in Urbana since childhood."

"Maybe he's not the real Gowdie anymore. He might have shapeshifted into Gowdie's form," Alice said.

"Only jinn can shapeshift. Wizards can't," Naveed yawned as if bored.

"OK, so O'Crowly is working with Gowdie," Alice said.

"Yes, and the O'Crowly working with him is Puck. I don't want it to be true, but it obviously is what happened," Naveed said, like he was tired of repeating.

"I thought you said Puck wasn't that good a mage and your magic was unbreakable," Alice said.

Naveed sat up and looked at Alice from over the back of the sofa. "It was unbreakable," he said in almost a roar. Then he looked away, mumbling, "So it probably was a higher level mage."

"I'm thinking we should go talk to Gowdie. Maybe he'll divulge something about the identity of this high-level mage he's working for," Alice said.

"I might be able to persuade him to talk." Naveed stood up. He narrowed his eyes and smiled in an absolutely devilish grin.

"That's actually a great idea, but you're going as the cat," Alice said, unphased by his jinn form, which would have scared her to death a month ago.

"I can't be as persuasive as a cat," Naveed said, his voice close to whining.

"He thinks I'm a high-level mage. How about I be the persuasive one?" Alice said, walking to the door.

"Fine, but I get to growl and maybe give him a scratch or two," Naveed said, following.

"Not unless it's necessary," Alice said.

At the door, Naveed said, "You didn't write anything

on your whiteboard?" Naveed pointed at the wall behind him.

"Just leave it," Alice said.

"Are you sure?" Naveed asked, simultaneously using his magic to make the abandoned blue marker write the words "Alice loves Baz" in the empty space.

"You are so annoying," Alice said flatly, and they headed for the police station.

TWENTY-TWO

Guilty Gowdie

A lice stopped at the doors of the police station, took a deep breath, and entered. Signing in took two minutes. She spotted Ron in a second.

"Officer Knight," she called out. It seemed odd to call him anything less formal in his workplace. Ron saw her and waved her over. Alice walked back to his desk. He offered her a seat, but Alice was too excited to take it, so they both stood.

"Before you say anything: The hex was real. The doctors are unable to do anything about it," Ron said.

"She really doesn't remember what happened to her?" Alice asked.

"Nothing, conveniently," Ron said.

"You still think she's guilty?"

"I think she had an accomplice, who conveniently erased her memory to keep himself out of trouble."

Alice ignored that he was referring to Baz. "I think she's innocent," Alice said.

"She could be. But Charlotte did have that briefcase of

poisons, so we have a right to detain her while we investigate that," Ron said.

"About that, I was wondering if I could speak to Gowdie," Alice said. She glanced briefly at Naveed, who had made himself comfortable on Ron's chair.

"You have some kind of proof against him?" Ron asked.

"I have a theory," Alice said.

"Alice, I appreciate that you found Charlotte and that you're interested in helping—"

"I know I'm not an officer, but I–"

"Quite frankly, I'm not even sure that–no, it's too ridiculous, never mind," Ron said.

"Now you have to tell me," Alice said.

"We got another tip about a non-mage pretending to be Talented in Magic Row," Ron said. Naveed lifted his front paws to the desk in full alert, ready to pounce if needed. But Ron wasn't attacking. He couldn't even look Alice in the eye as he said, "I know it's not you, you're an Adelcraft, but you seem to have non-mage friends like that museum director–"

"He has nothing to do with—how do you even know about that?" Alice asked.

"I know everything that happens in Magic Row— that's my job. If you talk to people outside this community about magic, there are consequences," Ron said, lowering his voice even though the station was hexed for the non-mage officers not to hear any talk about magic.

Alice knew she ought to keep her fiery nature out of a police station. Still, she couldn't help saying, "Maybe you should consider that your anonymous tipster might be misleading you on purpose. Or the fact that he called you from a non-mage tip-line," Alice said.

The sound of someone clearing his throat interrupted

Alice's and Ron's conversation. Mr. Pierce, the late Delvaux's butler stood patiently beside Alice, waiting to speak.

"Yes?" Ron asked.

Mr. Pierce took off his hat and ran a hand through his well-styled blond hair. "Sir, Miss, if I may interrupt," he said.

"Of course, Mr. Pierce, what can I do for you?" Ron asked.

"Well, sir, this came in from the council as a priority message addressed to Ms. Fowler. I thought it prudent to bring it to you."

Ron took a letter opener from his desk and slid it along the top of the white envelope. Silver sparks flew as he sliced the paper. Alice gasped. Naveed lifted his paws to the desk, peering at the now-open letter.

"That's another person's mail. You can't open it," Alice said.

Ron held the letter opener up, pointing to a pentagram insignia on the handle. "The mage council issued a warrant. If they hadn't, this wouldn't have worked to break the magic protecting the message."

Ron slid the letter out of the envelope. His eyes darted back and forth as he read. Alice tried spying past Ron's elbow, but he was too tall for her to see what was in his hands.

Alice wanted to ask what it said but didn't want to risk Ron's wrath. Ron turned to his left and put out an arm, stopping a passing officer.

"Release Ms. Fowler," he ordered. The officer nodded and walked back to the holding rooms.

"What did the letter say?" Alice couldn't help it. She had to know, and Ron should have expected she'd ask.

Ron looked at her sideways, questioning whether it was

worth it to snap at her again. He relented. "It seems Ms. Fowler was not anyone's accomplice. She was here in Urbana to turn Gowdie in for his black market operations."

"The potions in her briefcase, they were to test Gowdie's inventory. This explains it," Alice said.

"It doesn't explain everything," Ron said, giving Alice a look.

He wasn't going to talk about the poison in front of Mr. Pierce. That would only lead to more gossip and speculation. Alice kept her lips sealed, too.

"So, is Ms. Fowler free to leave? Because she promised to take me on as her butler—"

"Yes, she's free to go. I guess I can remand her into your custody, Mr. Pierce?" Ron asked.

"I have errands to run…but, yes, sir, I suppose I could take her with me," Mr. Pierce said.

"Not in her current condition. What if she wanders away? With no memory, she might not find her way back to you. Why don't you take her to Many Treasures? She can stay with us while you run your errands. You can pick her up on your way home," Alice volunteered.

"I'd appreciate that. Thank you," Mr. Pierce said, nodding his head and smiling.

Ms. Fowler appeared with an officer guiding her to Ron. Ron stepped back. "Ms. Fowler, you are cleared of all charges. We apologize for any inconvenience."

"This way, Ms. Fowler," Mr. Pierce guided her to the front desk.

"Why didn't you go with them?" Ron asked.

"I'm here to see Gowdie, remember?" Alice folded her arms.

Ron rubbed his temple like he was tired of arguing. "Fine. He's free to talk to you. He just made bail, and so did my sister, so I'll be taking the rest of the day off," Ron said. The exasperation in his voice was hard to miss. Ron pointed to the back of the station, where Oliver Gowdie was talking to a clerk. He signed some paperwork, and the clerk handed him an envelope of his personal effects.

"They're out already? That was fast," Alice commented.

"We only have two mage judges, but one cleared her schedule for the hearings," Ron said.

Alice understood why they'd prioritize rich and influential mages like Oliver Gowdie and Titania Knight. She couldn't fathom why the judge had let Mr. Gowdie— a man running a black-market— go free, no matter how high the bail. Titania was a different story. Baz was too kind to press charges.

Alice had moments where she felt sorry for Titania. She was on the verge of one when Titania walked into view. She evaded the officers guiding her to the property clerk's station, heading to her brother's desk with a scowl on her face. Ron groaned.

"Excuse me," he said, grabbing his jacket off the back of his chair and heading off a confrontation between his sister and the officers.

Alice stayed where she was since Gowdie had to pass Ron's desk to exit the station. She looked at Naveed, still on his hind legs, reaching his front paws up, peering over the desk in adorable cat-jinn fashion.

"Go to Many Treasures and make sure everything's all right with Charlotte there," Alice commanded.

Naveed meowed his disapproval, but he disappeared.

Meanwhile, Gowdie made his way through the station. He was looking down to put his watch on, so he didn't see Alice until she was blocking his path. He tried side-stepping, but she moved in tandem. Finally, he looked up.

"Not you again," Mr. Gowdie rolled his eyes as he clasped his gold watch around his wrist.

"Nice to see you, too," Alice said.

"Out of my way." Mr. Gowdie tried stepping around Alice again.

"I don't see why you're so sour. You got out," Alice said.

"You think that's a good thing? It wasn't my choice. I'm better off in prison," Mr. Gowdie said.

Alice followed him as he walked through the police station. In part that was to avoid Titania, whom Alice could see nearing. They got to the front, and Mr. Gowdie stopped to sign more paperwork.

"Why would you want to stay in jail?" Alice asked.

"You're kidding? Your buddy didn't tell you?" Mr. Gowdie pointed with his pen toward Ron's desk.

"No. Are you going to tell me, or should I hear it from the grapevine tomorrow?" Alice asked.

"You'd better not, or I'll be dead tomorrow," Mr. Gowdie said. He handed the papers and pen back to the clerk and walked outside, stopping a moment to take in a breath of fresh air.

"You turned on someone," Alice said.

"Someone dangerous," Mr. Gowdie agreed. He began walking.

"Who?" Alice asked, following him down the street.

Gowdie shook his head. "If I tell you that and word gets back to him, I'm dead."

"I won't tell, I promise," Alice said.

"Ha! Like I believe that," Mr. Gowdie said.

"What if I give you something in return? I...uh, I can get you a—"

"Don't bother. I won't tell you." He stopped and looked at Alice, adding, "But just to see your panicked expression for my amusement, I'll tell you this: You might wish I had my black-market magic available when the real villain shows up in Urbana." Mr. Gowdie resumed his exit.

Alice increased her pace. "You know about O'Crowly," she said.

Mr. Gowdie stopped abruptly, causing Alice to bump into him. He pivoted, then moved forward, cornering Alice against the wall without touching her, "How do you—never mind how you know. Don't ever repeat that."

"I need to know who—" Alice began.

Mr. Gowdie interrupted, "I'm serious. If you won't keep quiet to save my life, do it for Urbana. If you talk about this, you're going to cause a panic."

"But you're going to testify about—"

"I've already given my testimony in a closed hearing with select members of the council. There's no trial. There is no need to rattle the town." Mr. Gowdie held his stare until Alice nodded. Then he turned around and headed toward the bus stop, leaving Alice with her back against the wall, stunned and staring at him getting away.

"There you are!"

Alice closed her eyes as if squeezing her lids closed would make Titania go away. It was too late. Titania was two feet from Alice and might have swung a fist if her brother hadn't caught her forearm.

"Titania, let it go," Ron said.

With her free arm, Titania pointed her index finger at Alice. "You think you can have him, but you can't. You can't have something that's mine. Just because your an Adelcraft doesn't make you any better than a Knight.

"Titania." Ron took a harsher tone and pulled her back.

"Why don't *you* date her?" Titania pointed to her brother. She turned back to Alice and said, "You want to date my brother, that's fine. Go ahead. But leave Baz alone."

"No," Alice said in almost a knee-jerk reaction. She was too fired up to realize how that might add fuel to the already hot gossip spreading around Urbana about her, but she said, "You can't tell me what to do, and you certainly can't tell Baz who to see— not after what you did."

"Oh, boy," Ron muttered.

"You little—" Titania screeched as she took another swing. Ron picked her up by the waist and jerked her back before she could injure Alice.

"Are you OK?" Ron asked, looking at Alice while still holding his flailing sister.

Alice nodded. She could feel the heat in her cheeks, but could also see the tears in Titania's eyes, which calmed Alice down.

"I'm sorry," Alice said, her voice softening. "You made a mistake, and it cost you. I can't change that. But were you really living the life you wanted?"

"I had everything," Titania said, through tears.

"You weren't happy," Alice said in as kind a voice as she could.

"Come on," Ron set his sister down and gently guided her to his car. She sobbed the whole way.

Alice felt like crying, too. Titania had a breakdown, Gowdie turned on O'Crowly, and Alice was no closer to finding Perseus's killer and getting Baz off the hook. Worse than all that, Alice had no doubt left that O'Crowly was in town, and she had no clue to his identity.

TWENTY-THREE

Restored Recollection

Alice brought Charlotte inside Many Treasures. Mrs. Kinjo put up some tea, and Alice guided her to the sofa to rest.

"This is a nice place," Charlotte said, clearly not loving the décor. She must have been used to nicer things. Though, by "nicer," most people meant new and untouched, lifeless pieces of furniture with no backstories to tell, which was nothing like Alice's definition. Alice ignored the half-meant compliment and sat on the sofa chair across from Charlotte. Naveed, in cat-jinn form, jumped onto the arm-rest beside her.

"What do you remember?" Alice asked.

"Everything is hazy," Charlotte said, putting a hand over her eyes wearily.

Alice scooted to the edge of her seat and said, "Please, just try to remember."

Charlotte stared at the wall behind Alice, looking at nothing, concentrating. A minute later, she shook her head. "It's no use. It's all jumbled. I don't know what happened." She was on the verge of tears.

Alice reached out and touched Charlotte's hand. "It's all right. I'll go bring out something for you to eat, OK?" Alice walked into the kitchen, passing by Mrs. Kinjo and her tray of tea and biscuits. As Mrs. Kinjo poured two cups in the living room, Alice was left alone with Naveed. Alice kept her voice low as she asked her cat-jinn, "Can't you do something?"

Naveed transformed into a human, one whose body language signaled *"No,"* from his feet firmly planted on the floor to his hand, making a stop-sign signal in front of him. "I can't undo a memory hex. At best, I'd recover images that would just confuse her," Naveed said.

"Could it hurt her?" Alice asked.

"That depends on her. If she's strong and wants answers, then maybe she'll be fine. But if she's scared, it might drive her insane," Naveed said.

"Define 'might,'" Alice said.

"Alice!" Naveed whisper-yelled.

"All right, all right, no memory spells. What about just guiding her? You know, lending Charlotte a little magic to help her sort through her memories," Alice said.

"She did say her memories were 'jumbled.' I might be able to help her sort them."

Alice grabbed Naveed's hand. "Come with me— in human form."

"I have to be your brother again?" Naveed said.

"We can say I called you for help. Maybe she'll let you try," Alice said.

"Oh, fine, but I can't come out of the kitchen or they'll know I was the cat," Naveed said.

Alice walked back into the living room. Naveed appeared at the stairs, introducing himself as Alice's brother. Mrs. Kinjo looked between. Alice made the correction to *"half-brother,"* but Mrs. Kinjo kept giving him a suspicious, side-ways stare.

"Excuse me. I should attend to the cat," Mrs. Kinjo said. She got up and walked to the kitchen. As she passed Alice, she whispered, "I'm assuming the cat is your 'brother?'"

"Yep," Alice whispered back.

Mrs. Kinjo shook her head and continued at her slow pace out of the room.

Alice smiled nervously at Charlotte. "Naveed is good at fixing memory hexes," she explained.

Charlotte stared at Alice as if trying to read her.

"Ms. Fowler, I'd like to try to jog your memory, if you'll permit me," Naveed said.

"They had a doctor who already tried," Charlotte said.

"My magical talent exceeds theirs," Naveed replied. Catching Alice's eye, he added, "Or so I'm told. If you let me, I think I can undo your hex."

Naveed walking to the back of the couch. Charlotte's eyes followed Naveed. By the time he reached the space behind her, she had nodded and turned back around. Naveed placed his fingers on each other temples and guided her head to the back of the sofa. Charlotte closed her eyes.

"Breathe," Naveed said. After a minute, he instructed, "Try to recall where you were yesterday."

"I don't …yes, the estate…I remember. I went to the estate for the reading."

"That was three nights ago. Do you remember the night after that?"

Charlotte's forehead creased as she concentrated. "Downtown," she said.

"Good," Naveed said. "Where specifically?"

"The Essential Mage," Charlotte said.

Naveed and Alice exchanged smiles. "What happened at The Essential Mage?"

"I—I found black magic," Charlotte said.

"And then what happened?" Naveed asked.

"The lawyer. I made an appointment to write out a deal for Gowdie to give up his secret investor for less jail time," Charlotte said.

"You went to a criminal lawyer?" Alice asked.

"Chocolates!" Charlotte said, suddenly smiling. "He gave me a chocolate— cherry-flavored," Charlotte said.

Naveed looked at Alice as if this whole thing were a waste of time. Still, he continued in a gentle tone, "Not the food. We need to know where you went next, who was with you. Things like that."

"I don't remember, everything is fuzzy after that," Charlotte said. Charlotte sat upright and opened her eyes. She fumbled through her purse, searching for something. "Oh, where is the form? And where is my briefcase? He took my briefcase!" Charlotte sat up, looking nervously around the room.

"It's OK, the police have it. It's safe and so are you," Alice said.

"Not from him," Charlotte replied, her voice shaking.

"Who, Gowdie?" Naveed asked.

"I saw his face." Charlotte paled at the memory.

"You saw O'Crowly?" Alice asked softly.

Charlotte burst into tears. Mrs. Kinjo came into the room to see what was going on. She shot confused glances at Alice and Naveed and then sat beside Charlotte, putting an arm around her. "There, there, you're fine," Mrs. Kinjo said. Alice tried her best innocent look and hurried into the kitchen. Naveed followed.

"Congratulations, O'Crowly hexed her," Naveed said.

"But if he was trying to get Charlotte to forget about

the black magic, he'd have to hex the lawyer too. The lawyer might be in danger. Do you think it was Tom?" Alice asked.

"Charlotte did say he had chocolates," Naveed said.

"Why would Tom take the chocolates off of Perseus's desk? That makes no sense," Alice said.

"Maybe he gave the chocolates to Perseus in the first place," Naveed said.

Alice's eyes widened. "There was poison in the chocolate," she said.

"If Charlotte ate one, then it's not poisoned. Losing memory is a hex not a poison and other than her memory, Charlotte is fine," Naveed said.

"You took a caramel right?" Alice smiled.

"So Tom is guilty? He's not O'Crowly. He's not even Talented," Naveed said.

"No, he's not," Alice said, her brain connecting all the clues in sudden clarity. Alice took her phone out of her pocket and pulled up the text she'd ignored earlier.

"What is it?" Naveed asked.

"The will reading is subject to lawyer-client privilege. Charlotte Fowler was only interested in The Essential Mage. Titania was too vain to think about anything but what she'd get out of the will, and Baz would never tell anyone about what Merlin had stored in his safe," Alice said.

"You're back to how anyone knew about the wand?" Naveed asked.

"No one else knows about O'Crowly's possessions. You heard Gowdie. He said even talking about O'Crowly would stir up a panic. So how did Tom's client know?" Alice asked.

"So, Tom's client is O'Crowly?" Naveed said.

"O'Crowly or not, he's guilty," Alice said. She started

dialing a number on her phone. "Get the chocolate, and I'll call Ron. Then you and I are going to see a lawyer about a client," Alice said.

Naveed was gone and back in seconds. Alice took only a few seconds to fire out, "Get to Tom Willow's office, now." Then she clicked off the phone before Ron could argue about returning to work on a day he'd taken off.

Alice and Naveed walked back to the living room. They couldn't just disappear in front of Mrs. Kinjo or that might be more magic than she could handle. And Charlotte was distrusting as it was, so leaving without saying good-bye may have distressed her.

On their way out, Alice reassured Charlotte. "Just rest. Mr. Pierce will be by soon to take you home."

"What about your cat?" Ms. Fowler asked. Even hexed, she was perceptive.

"He's not an ordinary cat," Alice replied. She and Naveed both grinned.

"Oh?" Charlotte raised an eyebrow.

"He's my familiar. He always knows where to find me." Alice smiled.

She breathed a sigh of relief while walking down the stairs. Even hexed, Charlotte seemed suspicious of everyone. As a member of the mage council, she could probably arrange for Alice to be hexed in a heartbeat. Thankfully, Alice was reasonably sure she'd fooled Charlotte into thinking she was a witch – this time.

"Last chance," Mr. Coulson greeted Alice downstairs.

"Pardon?" Alice asked, surprised not only by Mr. Coulson, but by Naveed's disappearance. She spotted him on the floor behind her. He had transformed into a cat before they had reached the landing.

"For the trip!" Mr. Coulson said. He held his arms out

wide, showing off his new pinstripe suit. "I'm leaving tonight."

"Right. For Egypt. I'm sorry, Mr. Coulson, I'm staying here," Alice said, she looked around the store, annoyed that Eric must have forgotten to lock the door after Many Treasures had closed for the day.

Mr. Coulson snapped his fingers disappointedly. "I don't suppose that Morgan boy would want to go on an adventure? Does he know about these antiques like you do?"

"No. Actually, Puck was looking forward to performing at your museum," Alice said.

"Oh, I do apologize for that! My secretary sometimes takes it upon herself to make my decisions for me. I'll talk to her."

"And Puck can do a show?"

"Of course," Mr. Coulson smiled. "Tell the boy we'll set it up as soon as I get back."

"When will that be?" Alice asked.

Mr. Coulson shrugged, "Depends on what I find."

"Or don't find?" Alice asked.

"That's your one imperfection, isn't it? Always the pessimist." Mr. Coulson chuckled.

"A realist," Alice said. "What are you looking for this time, anyway?" she asked, realizing that she hadn't actually inquired about the subject of the dig. He hadn't gone into details, so she took a guess, "A new dig site opened near one of the pyramids?

Mr. Coulson, put his hat on, saying, "Better: A hidden cavern near the Nile with carvings of the myths of the north."

"Jinn myths?" Naveed asked. Somehow he'd made it behind Mr. Coulson and transformed.

"Yes." Mr. Coulson turned around and laughed in

delight. "Most people wouldn't know that. Who are you?" Mr. Coulson asked. Naveed crossed his arms. Alice felt the sweat forming on her forehead. The long-lost, half-brother lie wasn't going to work on Mr. Coulson.

Alice went for a vague non-answer, "A relative. Have fun on your trip. Sorry that I can't be there," she said.

"I'm sorry, too. 'Till we meet again," Mr. Coulson said, shaking Alice's hand.

The moment he left, Naveed spun around. "You just let him go?"

"Why shouldn't I? And why are you transforming in plain sight?" Alice asked.

"He's going into a jinn city!"

"Relax, if they discovered cave drawings, it's been occupied by humans before. Besides, he said it was a new dig site, which means there are already people working there who set up the dig."

"Desecrating my people's history," Naveed said.

"Preserving it, trying to understand it," Alice said.

"They're untalented. They understand nothing." Naveed crossed his arms.

"We're not going to agree on this. Can you just get me to Tom's office?"

"It's a building full of Untalented," Naveed said.

"I don't want to delay any longer or Ron will be there before us," Alice said.

"Shame if that happens, I'd hate for him to miss out on all the fun," Naveed said, then he linked arms with Alice and went off to save the day.

TWENTY-FOUR

Legal Matters

I t all spun together like a spider's web. Tom's web of lies began with his lie about when he'd first learned of magic. It wasn't after Liza told him. Long before that, he'd struck a deal with his very first client. Client 01 was O'Crowly. Tom had agreed to help O'Crowly set up a black magic market in Urbana, and he recruited Oliver Gowdie to run it. But it was a long jump from there to murdering an old wizard in his sleep. Except that old wizard had found Gowdie's red ledger and was black-mailing him and in danger of discovering O'Crowly's presence.

The poison found in Perseus's system had to be non-magical— to throw the mage community off. That meant Tom had to poison Perseus himself, and calling into the tip line to misguide officers wasn't difficult for a corrupt lawyer to do.

Alice's suspicions were confirmed as she walked into Tom's office. Betsy, Tom's secretary, stopped Alice at the reception desk. Naveed, in cat form, jumped onto the counter, meowing at a box of chocolates – the same imported European kind Tom had brought to the party as a present.

"Mr. Willows is on a call, and there are no pets allowed," Betsy said, giving Naveed the side-eye.

"I'm afraid I have urgent business," Alice said, walking right past Betsy.

"I can make an appointment," Betsy said, trying to rush past her to the door. Naveed jumped and landed in front of her, almost causing her to trip and fall. For added measure, he transported Alice straight into Tom's office. Alice locked the door behind her.

Tom stood up straight, with the phone still in his hand. "I'll have to call you back," Tom said. He put down the receiver and smiled. "Alice, what a pleasant—"

"Give it up Tom, I know it was you," Alice said.

"I'm sorry, what's me?" He asked.

"You poisoned Perseus Delvaux and framed Baz," Alice said.

Tom put his hands in his pockets, unintimidated. "Miss Adelcraft, I don't appreciate wild accusations. Baz is my client—"

"What better way to get his fingerprints? That broken pen you gave him at the will signing, which I thought was from some sleazy motel, was actually a shell of a syringe from the Rose Hospital."

"It might have been a pen from the Rose Hospital, but I'd hardly give a client a syringe to write with," Tom said, chuckling.

"You did a little craft work to transform it into a pen. Then you gave it to Baz. When he gave it back, because it didn't work, you used your handkerchief to make sure there were only Baz's fingerprint on it. Later, you transformed it back into a syringe," Alice said.

"A syringe pen? I'm not a doctor, but as far as I know, those two things look very different," Tom said.

"Not so different that through craft work or magic you couldn't transform it," Alice said.

"Miss Adelcraft, I'm aware my wife told you I'm not magical. What, am I secretly Talented?" Tom asked.

"No. But your #1 client is at least a level nine. Charlotte Fowler figured that out when she came to see you about cutting Gowdie a deal to find out the identity of Gowdie's secret investor. She found who he was, and she wasn't as happy to do his bidding as you were."

"You are imaginative! My #1 client is a prominent member of Urbana society," Tom said.

"He's a warlock named O'Crowly," Alice said.

"He doesn't go by that name now." Tom smiled sinisterly.

"I don't doubt it. He would need a cover to go unnoticed in Magic Row. What name is he using now?"

"Alice," Tom chided, softly, "You know I can't tell. That's client-attorney privilege. Everything he tells me is confidential."

"Including his plans for Urbana?"

"His plans aren't just for Urbana. He thinks bigger than that," Tom actually smiled.

Alice grimaced in disgust. "Whatever O'Crowly's plans are, they can't be good for an Untalented. Why are you working for him?"

Tom's smile wavered. For a moment, he looked like a man coming out of a spell as he replied, "You think I don't care about my family, but I do. That includes Liza, despite everything."

"Immunity," Alice realized. "That's what you get. Liza and the twins get to...what...survive this awful plan?" Alice asked.

"His plan isn't awful. It's just fair. Survival of the fittest, and I may be Untalented, but I am fit to do what is necessary," Tom said. He unbuttoned the top button on his collar.

"Your client, the one who wants the wand. He knows that the wand was O'Crowly's. Is that because he's a descendant?" Alice asked.

"I already told you I'm not at liberty to divulge-"

"Just stop with the lawyer-client privilege. If you won't tell me, then you'll tell Ron everything."

"I don't think you told an officer you were coming here today. And your jinn is pretty useless in here," Tom said. He pointed to various stone carving in the room, one on his desk, one above the filing cabinet, one on the window pane. "They're not for jinn specifically, but they might keep him from casting any new spells while he's in here."

"You want to test that theory?" Alice asked.

Tom's amusement grew, as did the smile on his face. "I'll answer out of pure kindness. Yes, my client is an O'Crowly."

"Who is he? How far has he infiltrated Urbana?" Alice asked. She had a million questions on the tip of her tongue.

"Oh, very far. In fact, I'd say he's just about the most powerful person in the city."

"Who is he?" Alice asked, more forcefully this time.

"I'll give you a hint– only because O'Crowly himself likes the game–" Tom reached into the top left-hand drawer of his desk.

Alice shot her hand out as if to spell him. Tom chuckled. "Oh, come on. I know you're not a witch."

Alice's eyes widened. "What?" she asked.

"I think you mean *'how do I know that,'* right? I know a lot of things about you, Alice Adelcraft." Tom took his hand out of the drawer, flicking a photograph across the desk. It landed facing Alice. She didn't remember the picture but recognized her parents and her five-year-old self smiling up at her. Tom continued, "Your father's heart attack, your mother's unfortunate death in a fire, I know all of it. And I know some things you don't know about yourself, like the purpose of the amulet on your neck."

Alice touched her necklace. "What purpose is that?" she asked.

Tom smiled, "I'll tell you what, I'll answer one question. You choose which: I can tell you the purpose of the amulet. Or I can reveal a secret about your parents that will change everything you thought you knew about yourself."

Alice watched him in startled silence. Grinning for ear-to-ear, Tom waited patiently for her to decide, not at all bothered by the hubbub outside. Ron was talking to Betsy, who was asking him not to come in.

"You might have to tell them to wait if you want an answer. If they come in, I'm not saying anything," Tom said.

"They can spell you to spill your secrets."

"Don't you think O'Crowly would have thought of that? They'd have to break through a myriad of spells first. And this," Tom unbuttoned the top of his shirt and pulled out a chain with a charmed stone dangling from it.

"Tell them to wait," Alice said to Naveed.

He disappeared, leaving her alone with Tom.

"Tell me about my parents," she said.

Tom's grin grew, showing all his teeth. "Somehow, I knew you'd choose that. You're still a poor little orphan at heart."

"Stop stalling," Alice said.

"And here I thought it was you biding your time until the police arrived."

"They're already here," Alice said. Truthfully, she hadn't called Ron, but she was glad he was here.

Tom's hand moved toward his necklace.

"Try anything, and I'll order the jinn to let Ron inside," Alice said.

Tom held his hand up, surrendering. "You win."

"My parents," Alice said.

"Which ones?" Tom asked.

"What do you mean 'which ones?'" As Alice grew angrier, her necklace glowed.

"The Adelcrafts or your real parents?" Tom asked. He enunciated the words as if each syllable were a blow.

It worked. Alice felt the wind knocked out of her chest. "If I'm not an Adelcraft, what am I?" Alice could barely summon her breath to ask the question. It came out as a whisper.

"Now, that is exactly the right question," Tom said.

Ron pounded on the door. "Police. We're coming in," he said.

Tom clutched the stone at his chest. "That's my cue." He closed his eyes and disappeared.

Ron burst through the door, wand drawn. He relaxed when he saw Alice alone. "You let him go?" he asked.

"I couldn't stop him. But I think I know where he's going," Alice said.

TWENTY-FIVE

Criminal Lawbreaker

R on cited the rulebook as the reason for not entering Liza's residence. Alice was not a police officer. Ron could arrest her for breaking and entering later. Naveed took her straight into the Willows' living room.

Hazel's and Zade's ears were pressed against the kitchen door, listening. They jumped on hearing the banging at the front door. Hazel saw Alice first.

"Al-"

"Shh." Alice held a finger to her mouth, quieting Hazel.

"What are you doing here? And Puck?" Zade whispered.

Alice swiveled around. "What–how–"

Puck put his hands up, "I saw Ron in the hall. I was visiting a friend. What's going on?"

"Visiting a friend? Never mind, we'll talk about that later," Alice said. She turned toward the kids. "Is your dad in there?"

Zade nodded, "They're fighting."

"He wants us to go somewhere with him, but Mom said no," Hazel said.

Ron pounded on the door again. "Police, I'm coming in." Ron appeared in the living room. Hazel and Zade rushed to his side. As they explained the situation, Alice opened the kitchen door.

"Liza, you don't understand!" Tom had his hand outstretched, pleading. The moment he saw Alice, he lunged to grab Liza.

Alice was closer, she pulled Liza into the living room. Liza stumbled, then screamed as Tom appeared behind her. Ron held the kids back.

"Just trust me. You and the kids have to come with me. He can keep us safe." Tom had his hands around Liza's waist, and an arm outstretched toward the kids, ushering them toward him. Ron grabbed them by the sleeves.

"Who?" Zade asked, struggling against Ron's grip.

"O'Crowly," Naveed answered between sharp teeth.

"No," Puck said, his skin paling to ghost-white terror.

Tom turned toward Puck. "He can protect you, too," he said.

"Protect us from what?" Hazel's voice shook.

"They don't need protection from their own people. They haven't done anything wrong, not like you," Alice said.

"This doesn't concern you, j-" Naveed knocked him back before he could say "jinn-keeper" or worse.

Tom's charmed stone glowed. A blow that should have knocked him out caused him to stumble. He grabbed at his collar, revealed several stone necklaces. Through a trembling hand, he grabbed a green one and pointed.

Puck shot at him this time, an invisible force knocking the stone from his hand.

"Give up," Naveed said.

He and Puck loomed over Tom. Ron reached to pull Tom into cuffs, only to be caught in the jaw by Tom's fist. Tom flung Ron into Naveed and cast a wild, untrained spell with a stone from around his neck. Green light bounced off a wall and straight toward Hazel. She shrieked.

Puck lunged forward, plunging them both to the ground. "Are you all right?" Puck asked, pulling himself off of Hazel in seconds. Zade and Liza rushed toward her as Puck offered her his hand. With his help, Hazel stood.

"Yeah, I'm fine," Hazel said.

"How could you? That is our daughter!" Liza screamed.

"I...I didn't mean to," Tom said. He stood still genuinely stunned and vulnerable. Ron took this as an opportunity to capture his suspect. He grabbed Tom's shoulder and pinned him against the wall.

"You're under arrest, you treacherous creep," Ron said.

Tom struggled against his grasp, turning and swinging at Ron. The two engaged in an all-out brawl– no magic involved. Tom hit Ron in the chest, Ron gave one back in the stomach and twisted Tom's arm. Tom gave a deafening cry, which should not have been heard by his children.

"Don't hurt him!" Zade screamed. Liza clutched her son's shoulder and tried to shield his eyes, but he jerked away, watching. Hazel watched, too, with tears running down her cheeks. This was their father, no matter what he'd done.

"Take them away," Naveed said.

"He's right, get to safety," Alice said, guiding Liza and the twins to the door.

"No! I want to stay," Zade argued.

"Watch out!" Puck screamed suddenly as Tom gained the upper hand. He knocked Ron back, but Ron still had a grip on his arm. Puck shot another blast of some invisible force that pushed Tom to the floor. Unfortunately, it also broke Tom free of Ron's grasp.

Tom quickly pulled at his chain, finding a yellow stone and clutching it. He began to disappear in front of their eyes. In a second, he was gone.

"No, you don't!" Naveed yelled. He grabbed at thin air and yanked hard.

Tom not only reappeared. Naveed had him by the shirt collar. Tom fell back, skidding against the floor and rolling. Ron pulled out his handcuffs and threw them, aiming his wand at the metal. The cuffs shot onto Tom's hand and clicked in place.

"Get those charmed stones off of him!" Ron ordered.

Puck obeyed, kneeling and ripping the ropes off Tom hard enough to give cause burn marks on his skin.

"Dad!" Zade jolted forward. Hazel caught his arm and held tight. "Ow! Let me go!" Zade yelled. He called out, "Dad!" again.

"Don't call him that. Our dad left three years ago," Hazel said. Her eyes shot daggers at Tom. "We don't have a father," she said.

Despite holding back sobs, Liza pulled her kids back. She guided them into another room and shut the door. Ron watched her go, the anguish clear on his face.

Ron turned to Tom, pulling him up roughly to his feet. "You have the right to remain silent," he began.

"This is an illegal arrest! You have no proof that I've done anything! " Tom said.

Naveed took the chocolate out of his pocket. "Oh gross, it was smushed in the fight," Naveed said, turning his pocket inside out. Only a little had squeezed out of the wrapper. For the most part, the chocolate was whole. Naveed handed the caramel to Alice.

She held up the chocolate caramel in her hand and asked, "Will a poisoned chocolate Tom gave Perseus as a gift work as proof?"

"Yes, it absolutely will," Ron said, clicking his fingers for an evidence bag to appear.

Naveed put on hand on Puck's arm, the other on Alice's. "He has it from here. Let's go."

"Wait," Alice said. When Ron finished the Miranda rights, he raised his wand, ready to transport himself and Tom to the police station. Alice stopped him. "He wasn't working alone," Alice said.

"Yeah, I got that. Are you sure it's O'Crowly, though?"

Alice looked at Tom, whose lips were firmly sealed together in a defiant smile. "I'm sure," she said.

Ron shook his head. "That's going to change things around here," he said. Tom's smile grew. Ron pushed him forward toward the door. He stopped in front of Puck. "That was some good work. You might have a future in law enforcement."

"Yeah, I don't know about that." Puck ran a hand through his hair, his cheeks turning red.

Turning to Alice, Ron said, "Don't worry. If Tom is working with O'Crowly, we'll get the information out of him." Ron walked Tom forward, the two disappearing as they went out through the doorway.

"I've got to get out of Urbana," Puck said. He tried to walk away, but Naveed's hold on him was firm.

"Puck, we know who you are," Alice said.

Puck's jaw fell. "And? Are you going to tell Ron?" he asked.

"Ron already knows. He's known since you got to town," Alice said.

"And he's telling people?" Puck looked like a cornered mouse, ready to run before being caged.

Alice put a hand on his arm. "I'm the only person he told, and only because he knows the doesn't make a difference to me."

When the words sank in, Puck let out a wry laugh. "And he still thinks I should go into law enforcement?"

"You do have a future here, if you want it," Alice reassured him.

"But I don't understand." Puck rubbed his neck nervously. "You don't think I'm involved in this? I mean, it's an O'Crowly that's threatening the town."

"It's not you, and we know that." Alice put a hand on Puck's shoulder. Puck's eyes began to tear. He blinked and licked his lips, holding the emotion back.

"Who else knows?" Puck asked when he'd regained composure.

"No one," Naveed said.

"And we're going to keep it that way. Your secret is safe with us," Alice said.

"Now, can we go home?" Naveed asked.

"Yeah," Puck smiled. "Let's go home."

"Sure thing," Alice said. She reached into Puck's jacket and pulled out the diamond bracelet she saw dangling from the corner. "Right after you return this."

"I found that," Puck said.

"In whose apartment?" Alice asked.

Puck smiled. "All right, you got me. But I promise you this was going to be the last time. My friends dared me to–"

"Puck!" Alice said.

"OK, I'll put it back," Puck said.

"We'll put it back," Alice said. She linked one arm with him, the other with Naveed.

"Daria's place?" Naveed asked, eyeing Puck with anger as Puck shifted them to a posh apartment.

"The estate sale is tomorrow and I– I didn't know you knew her. Sorry. I really am," Puck said, changing tone when he saw Alice's disappointed look. He laid the bracelet back down and looked at Alice, a mix of hope and fear on his face. "You're not going to trust me again, are you?"

Alice sighed. "I promised I'd give you as many chances as you need. You can earn back my trust in time," Alice said.

"How long are we talking?" Puck asked.

"I don't know. How about after Ron swears you in as an officer?" Alice said.

"So, never?" Puck asked.

Naveed shook his head. He grabbed Alice and Puck by the shoulders, and the three went home. In this case, even for Alice, "home" would always mean Many Treasures.

TWENTY-SIX

Further Suspicion

"No, that's not how you do it. Here," Alice said, laughing as she fixed Puck's display in the window.

Alice repositioned the sign for the new antique wands, courtesy of Ms. Fowler, out of appreciation for helping her regain her memory. The shop was again filled with customers, and the gossip today was all in Alice's favor.

"I heard you saved the day?" Eric asked after Vestra had come in for a visit and left.

"I guess," Alice said.

"I had a little hand in it, too. I don't like to brag, but I don't think they would've caught Tom without me," Puck said.

"Anyway, I also heard you have a brother?" Eric raised an eyebrow.

Alice glanced at Naveed, or fluffy, the cat, and back at Eric, who had known her well enough to call that bluff. "Yeah," she said. She walked around the counter as nonchalantly as she could manage and whispered, "I'll explain later."

"Well, I guess I should be grateful he was there looking

out for you since I've kind of always thought of you as *my* little sister," Eric said. He reached out and ruffled her hair like he'd done when she was a teen.

"Stop, you know I hate that!" Alice said.

The front door opened just then. Alice came hair-covered-face to face with Baz. Alice quickly adjusted her curls, not so accidentally elbowing Eric in the shoulder at the same time. She ignored his "ow" and prayed that her hair still looked as good as it had in the mirror that morning.

"Alice," Baz said.

"Hi," Alice replied like a schoolgirl meeting her crush. She took a breath and tried again.

"I heard–"

"I have to–"

They spoke at the same time. Baz waited, but Alice said, "Go ahead."

"I have to thank you. I doubt the case would have been resolved so quickly, if at all, if not for you."

"I'm sure Ron could have–" Alice paused, noticing a man with salt and pepper hair entering through the shop's side door. "Baz, it's the man who asked for a wand earlier," Alice whispered.

Baz's eyes slid sideways, subtle in their perception of the man. Then he looked again, raised a hand and waved. The man waved back, smiling.

"Good morning, Mr. Smythe," Baz said.

"You know him?" Alice asked.

"I would think everyone does. He's the owner of Spell-binders," Baz replied.

"The mage repair shop?" Alice's cheeks reddened, and she put a hand to her forehead. The whole conversation played out differently in her head now. "'*An old wand, maybe something that needs extra care,*' that's what he said. He meant something he could fix up as part of his shop's services." Alice recalled aloud.

Puck laughed from behind the counter. "You guys talking about Mr. Smythe? I doubt he's O'Crowly pretending to be a spellbinder mage. He's been in Urbana for like twenty years," Puck said.

"I wouldn't rule anything out. But, I would leave the investigation to Ron. If it is O'Crowly, it would be best not to put yourself in his way," Baz said.

"I think I've proven I can handle myself," Alice said.

"I'd rather you didn't," Baz said.

"Why? Are you worried about me?" Alice asked, half-teasing, half-hoping it was true.

"Yes," Baz said simply. Alice's heart skipped a beat, especially with his blue eyes boring into her soul. He continued, "I'm worried for you, for Merlin, for Urbana. Everything is going to change."

"Ron said that, too," Puck said.

As if realizing he and Alice were not alone, Baz stopped leaning in close enough for Alice to smell his after-shave, spiced and warm to her delight. He straightened and replied, "It's true. A warlock like Gowdie is a nuisance; one like O'Crowly is a serious threat."

"I understand that Lester O'Crowly was a level ten wizard, but how do we know this descendant is so skilled? Talent doesn't always run in families," Alice said, speaking from experience.

"The O'Crowlys were rigorous in their pursuit of greatness. They taught their children to reach level eight by the time they were eighteen years old. In theory, they were all creator mages— though they were forbidden to study under any creator mages in the world.

"You keep using past tense," Alice noted.

"They've been cast out of most mage communities,

fallen from positions of high status. I haven't heard anything about them for two generations."

"Because they're all temperamental drunks with delusions of grandeur," Puck muttered. Realizing Baz was staring at him, he added, "Probably. I mean, what else could they be, right?"

"Puck, could you excuse us, please?" Baz asked, turning and guiding Alice toward the side door.

"Sure." Puck picked up a magazine only to put it down a second later as a customer approached the counter.

Baz opened the side door, extending his arm for Alice to take. She felt odd walking arm in arm with Baz. A warmth filled her body as she slid her hand around his elbow. As they stepped through the doorway, Baz shifting them out of the alley. The red bricks were replaced with the crimson of roses. Lush green grass replaced the pavement and yellow tulips, purple chrysanthemums, and more littered the field of view. Baz had brought her to his garden, Alice realized.

A few steps past the garden, he brought her to a double door and into a library. This one was small, cozy even with a wall of books, a safe with two lions holding the lock and two sofa chairs, each with their own end tables. Between the seats lay, instead of a fireplace, a lotus flower fountain. Bamboo plants and bonsai trees added to the zen-like atmosphere.

"Looks like Rhys' taste," Alice said, having been to Merlin's shadow.

"Merlin's space within my space," Baz explained.

"But you take care of the bonsai?" Alice asked, smiling.

"Actually, I was hoping you would care for them while I'm gone," Baz said.

Alice's smile vanished. "You're leaving?"

Baz walked to a bookshelf, pulling a cloth off of a crystal ball. He waved a hand, and an end table slid between the two sofa chairs. He and Alice took their seats and stared.

"I've been in regular contact with Merlin until yesterday when all I could see was this image."

Alice stared into the crystal, all she could see were ripples. A river, maybe? Then the view shifted, and Alice could see a hillside. The image closed in on an opening in the mound.

"A cave?" Alice asked.

"It may be an entrance to a jinn settlement. I can't be certain, but whatever it is, my vision doesn't extend past the entrance," Baz said.

"You think Merlin is in there?" Alice asked.

"That's what I have to find out. Hex and I are leaving tonight."

"Leaving Urbana with an O'Crowly lurking around?"

"Our best chance is in having a level ten mage here with us," Baz answered.

Alice nodded.

"Are you a level 10 mage, Alice? I have to know."

Alice swallowed. "No," she said, her breath stuck in her chest.

"Nine, then. There had to be some reason Merlin entrusted his affairs to you?"

"I can't say why he chose me," Alice said. That was the truth.

"All right. I won't press you on it. I have responsibilities split between you, Ron, and Celeste, and I've notified the council about O'Crowly. If anything should happen while I'm gone, I can be back within a day."

"How do I reach you?" Alice asked.

"I'm not as traditional as Merlin." Baz handed Alice a

business card with a phone number. Interestingly, the card described Baz as a real estate proprietor. "I'm not sure how long I'll be gone. I wanted to say before I go, I…thank you. You had faith in my innocence, I have to admit I don't know why."

"I just knew it wasn't you."

"A truthsayer or…you had no other reason? No, forgive me, of course not. I'm glad we have a truthsayer in Urbana, especially now. It's a good fortune for us all," Baz said.

Alice's chest hitched again. Alice shook her head, trying for complete ignorance as to what he was implying. She clutched the amulet around her neck as if it might give her away. She had no ability to sense the truth in other people.

Baz stood. He lifted up the crystal ball and waved the end table back in place. When he'd replaced the crystal on the bookshelf, he extended his arm again. Alice could have gotten used to walking arm-in-arm with Baz, but it was over in a second as they stepped past the library doorway. Alice found herself back in the alleyway, the scent of fresh flowers replaced by the dumpster. She understood in one breath why the Magic Row customers were complaining.

Alice focused on Baz's spice-scented aftershave as she said goodbye. "Bring him home," Alice said.

"I will," Baz replied.

Home, Alice mused as Baz disappeared, *was where the magic was*, and there was no better place for Alice in all the world.

Now all that was left was for her to keep it safe.

Epilogue

I wish I could say that Baz returned home with Merlin, safe and sound. That they discovered O'Crowly and ended his evil plans– that is what happens in stories. But life is often different than stories. And, barring some event I cannot see in my crystal ball, Alice's life may very soon come to an end.

The Story Continues

Coming Soon
Book 4: Spellbinding Sales.

Go to astoriawright.com for more info on this series and others by the author.

www.ingramcontent.com/pod-product-compliance
Lightning Source LLC
Chambersburg PA
CBHW022017170626
46808CB00001B/449

* 9 7 8 1 9 4 9 4 5 3 3 2 4 *